PRAISE FOR DONNA GRANT'S BESTSELLING
ROMANCE NOVELS

"Time travel, ancient legends, and seductive romance are seamlessly interwoven into one captivating package."
    —*Publishers Weekly* on Midnight's Master

"Dark, sexy, magical. When I want to indulge in a sizzling fantasy adventure, I read Donna Grant."
    —Allison Brennan, *New York Times* bestseller

5 Stars! Top Pick! "An absolute must read! From beginning to end, it's an incredible ride."
    —*Night Owl Reviews*

"It's good vs. evil Druid in the next installment of Grant's Dark Warrior series. The stakes get higher as discerning one's true loyalties become harder. Grant's compelling characters and continued presence of previous protagonists are key reasons why these books are so gripping. Another exciting and thrilling chapter!"
    —*RT Book Reviews* on Midnight's Lover

"Donna Grant has given the paranormal genre a burst of fresh air..."
    —*San Francisco Book Review*

WILD RAPTURE

A CHIASSON STORY

DONNA GRANT

Dragon Fever (novella)

The Dragon King Coloring Book

Firestorm

Blaze

Dragon Burn

Constantine: A History (short story)

Heat (January 30, 2018)

Torched (June 2018)

DARK WARRIORS

Midnight's Master

Midnight's Lover

Midnight's Seduction

Midnight's Warrior

Midnight's Kiss

Midnight's Captive

Midnight's Temptation

Midnight's Promise

Midnight's Surrender (novella)

Dark Warrior Box Set

THE KINDRED

Everkin (novella)

Eversong (November 20, 2017)

Coming April 2018: Book 2

Coming December 2018: Book 3

———

CHIASSON SERIES

Wild Fever

Wild Dream

Wild Need

Wild Flame

Wild Rapture

———

LARUE SERIES

Moon Kissed

Moon Thrall

Moon Struck

Moon Bound (January 2018)

———

WICKED TREASURES

Seized By Passion

Enticed By Ecstasy

Captured By Desire

Wicked Treasures Box Set

A Dark Seduction

A Forbidden Temptation

A Warrior's Heart

DRUIDS GLEN

Dragonfyre (connected)

Highland Mist

Highland Nights

Highland Dawn

Highland Fires

Highland Magic

SISTERS OF MAGIC

Shadow Magic

Echoes of Magic

Dangerous Magic

Sisters of Magic Boxed Set

THE ROYAL CHRONICLES NOVELLA SERIES

Dragonfyre (connected)

Prince of Desire

Prince of Seduction

Prince of Love

Prince of Passion

Royal Chronicles Box Set

ANTHOLOGIES

The Pleasure of His Bed

(including *Ties That Bind*)

The Mammoth Book of Scottish Romance

(including *Forever Mine*)

Scribbling Women and the Real-Life Romance Heroes Who Love Them

1001 Dark Nights: Bundle Six (including *Dragon King*)

This is a work of fiction. All of the characters, organizations, and events portrayed in this novel are either products of the author's imagination or are used fictitiously.

PRONUNCIATIONS & GLOSSARY

GLOSSARY:

Andouille (ahn-doo-ee) & **Boudin** (boo-dan)
Two types of Cajun sausage. Andouille is made with pork while boudin with pork and rice.

Bayou (by-you)
A sluggish stream bigger than a creek and smaller than a river

Beignet (bin-yay)
A fritter or doughnut without a hole, sprinkled with powdered sugar

Cajun ('ka-jun)
A person of French-Canadian descent born or living along southern Louisiana.

Etoufee (ay-two-fay)

Tangy tomato-based sauce dish usually made with crawfish or shrimp and rice

Gumbo (gum-bo)
Thick, savory soup with chicken, seafood, sausage, or wild game

Hoodoo (hu-du)
Also known as "conjure" or witchcraft. Thought of as "folk magic" and "superstition". Some say it is the main force against the use of Voodoo.

Jambalaya (jom-bah-LIE-yah)
Highly seasoned mixture of sausage, chicken, or seafood and vegetables, simmered with rice until liquid is absorbed

Maman (muh-mahn)
Term used for grandmother

Parish
A Louisiana state district; equivalent to the word county

Sha (a as in cat)
Term of affection meaning darling, dear, or sweetheart.

Voodoo (vu-du) – New Orleans
Spiritual folkways originating in the Caribbean. New Orleans Voodoo is separate from other forms (Haitian Vodou and southern Hoodoo). New Orleans Voodoo puts emphasis on Voodoo Queens and Voodoo dolls.

Zydeco (zy-dey-coh)
Accordion-based music originating in Louisiana combined with

guitar and violin while combing traditional French melodies with Caribbean and blues influences

----

PRONUNCIATION:

Arcineaux (are-cen-o)
Chiasson (ch-ay-son)
Davena (dav-E-na)
Delia (d-ee-l-ee-uh)
Delphine (d-eh-l-FEEN)
Dumas (dOO-mah-s)
Lafayette (lah-fai-EHt)
LaRue (l-er-OO)

ACKNOWLEDGMENTS

A special thanks goes out to my family who lives in the bayous of Louisiana. Those summers I spent there are some of my most precious memories. I also need to send a shout-out to my team. Hats off to my editor, Chelle Olson, and cover design extraordinaire, Leah Suttle. Thank you for helping me get this story out!

Lots of love to my amazing kiddos - Gillian and Connor. Thanks for putting up with my hectic schedule and for talking plot lines. And a special hug for the Grant furbabies - Sheba, Sassy, Diego, and Sisko.

Last but not least, my readers. You have my eternal gratitude for the amazing support you show me and my books. Y'all rock my world. Stay tuned at the end of the story for the first sneak peek of *The Christmas Cowboy Hero*, the first book in my Heart of Texas series out October 31, 2017. A Christmas story on Halloween. How much better can life get?!

Xoxo
Donna

PROLOGUE

March

Something was wrong. Terribly wrong.

Riley squeezed her eyes closed to shield them from the blinding light as she came awake on her side. She attempted to sit up, but was wracked with pain all through her body.

What the hell had happened?

She finally managed to open her eyes to find herself on the floor of a room. There were boards placed over the windows, many of them smashed or rotting. The curtains that were barely hanging on had fabric ripped and were so filthy the color was indiscernible. Dirt, debris, and broken furniture littered the floor.

Riley gritted her teeth and pushed up onto one hand. Images of the battle she'd fought in New Orleans with Minka and her cousins, the LaRues, flooded her. Fear threatened to swallow her whole, but she refused to allow it. Because she knew who had her.

Delphine.

If the priestess thought she could make her cower, Delphine

was in for a rude awakening. Riley was a Chiasson, a hunter of the supernatural, one who was ready and willing to fight anything. Delphine was just another evil monster that had to be taken down.

"Bring your worst!" Riley shouted to whoever might be listening—or watching.

She climbed to her feet and dusted off her hands, her gaze scanning the room for a way out. Then she whispered, "I'll be ready for you."

May
Lyons Point, Louisiana

*E*vil had come to town. There might not be a physical body, but Marshall Ducet knew it was there all the same. He'd left New Orleans because of it.

He snorted as he drove down Highway 13 on patrol. Somewhere out in the universe, someone was laughing, all because Marshall had unknowingly chosen to relocate to another paranormal hotspot.

If he thought New Orleans was bad with all the various factions of the supernatural—werewolves, witches, djinn, vampires, and Voodoo—it had nothing on Lyons Point and the surrounding area.

The sleepy little town looked idyllic. Right up until he discovered that some unknown force drew the paranormal here. And there was a family—the Chiassons—who hunted the evil and kept everyone safe.

Marshall got involved with the Chiassons after arriving at a murder caused by a Voodoo priestess, and once he knew of the hunters, he gladly helped out when he could.

He slowed and turned down a road. The sun was bright in the cloudless sky, allowing the temperatures to come close to ninety degrees. The previous sheriff had been killed after succumbing to the paranormal, so as acting sheriff, Marshall spent most of his time driving around and helping those in need. Though there was still the occasional robbery and B&E.

And then there were the murders.

Few and far between, the killings nine times out of ten were supernatural. Marshall had quickly learned how to tell them apart. Mostly because, if any of the Chiassons were there, it was supernatural.

Marshall turned down the crepe myrtle-lined drive. He was paying his daily visit to the four Chiasson brothers and their women to see if there was any word on their only sister.

When Riley had gone missing in New Orleans while fighting Delphine, a Voodoo priestess, the Chiasson brothers were at first in shock. Then came the anger. Not that he could blame them. Marshall suspected he would act very much the same in a similar situation, but it was all a guess since he was an only child.

He had an inkling that the chaos of the Chiasson home was what drew him back time and again. He'd always dreamed of having siblings, and while his wish never came true, he could briefly live it when he was around the hunters.

Marshall parked the patrol car and turned off the ignition. He met his gaze in the rearview mirror and sighed. Riley hadn't been alone during the battle. In fact, she'd been standing along-side her cousins, the LaRues—who happened to be werewolves and the ones who kept the factions within New Orleans playing nice with each other and the humans.

The LaRues had scoured the city. And then the Chiassons

had joined in the search before doing one of their own. And still, there wasn't a single sign of Riley. It was like she'd disappeared.

Grabbing his Stetson, Marshall exited the car and stood. He set the hat on his head and pushed the car door closed as he headed toward the front porch. On his way, he saw movement in the building off to the side of the main house. He altered his direction and came to the doorway of the large boat shed that had various metal cages within to hold supernatural creatures.

The cages had been used fairly recently with Kane LaRue after he was cursed by Delphine to kill Ava Ladet in retaliation for her dad, Jack, pissing off the priestess. Luckily, one of the Chiasson brothers, Lincoln, had taken a fancy to her, and the Chiassons were able to intercept their cousin before he could carry out the curse.

As Marshall looked at the cages, he recalled how close Ava had come to dying, and how both the Chiassons and the LaRues would've been impacted by her death.

For one, had Kane killed her—or any human—he would've remained in werewolf form for eternity.

Then there was Lincoln. He would've lost the love of his life.

It was the quick thinking of the Chiassons and how well they worked together that stopped the Voodoo priestess out for revenge. And it brought the two families back together again after drifting apart.

Now, however, it seemed as if Delphine had taken the ultimate revenge by kidnapping Riley. Because while no one had any evidence that it was Delphine, there was no one else who'd made it clear they would get their vengeance on the two families.

Marshall's gaze went to the eldest Chiasson, Vincent. He stood with his back to everyone, gazing out the open door of the shed to the bayou beyond. Vin's dark hair fell in waves to his shoulders.

"Hey," Christian said.

Marshall gave a nod to the middle brother and met his bright blue eyes—a family trait for the Chiassons and LaRues. It made Marshall recall the only time he'd seen Riley. She'd been on her way back to New Orleans. She'd walked from the large, white plantation house as he'd driven up.

Her steps had been assertive, her smile confident, while her gaze dared anyone to get in her way. He'd seen the dimple in her left cheek as he leaned against his hood and watched her drive away.

It was a good thing they hadn't spoken because Marshall was certain he wouldn't have been able to form words. Riley Chiasson wasn't just stunningly beautiful, she was also a force to be reckoned with. Though, it was her beauty that most people saw—not that Marshall could blame them.

She was tall and lithe with just the right amount of curves. Her long hair was so dark it was nearly black as it fell in waves down her back. She sported the same piercing blue eyes as the rest of her kin, but it was the dimple in her left cheek that he loved most of all.

"Any news?" Marshall asked.

Lincoln shook his head of dark hair and continued sharpening his knives.

Beau put away his shotgun and said, "Linc wants to return to New Orleans to do another search."

"We can't," Christian said. "Not with the nest of vampires that arrived last week. We can't leave those who count on us."

Linc spun around to face his younger brother. "And what about Riley? It's been weeks, Christian! Weeks! We don't have any idea what horrors Delphine has inflicted on her."

"Solomon, Myles, Kane, and Court continue to look for her," Christian argued. "And if you think it's easy for me to stay here and do nothing, then you're a bigger dick than I thought."

In a split second, Beau was between his brothers, a hand on each of their chests. "This isn't doing Riley any good."

"Beau's right," Marshall said. "I'm not taking sides because I don't think I could stay here if it was my sister, but at the same time, Lyons Point needs this family. And from what all of you have told me, no one knows New Orleans like the LaRues."

"Then why haven't they found her?" Vin asked without turning around.

All three brothers swiveled their heads to Vin. Beau dropped his arms and turned to face his eldest brother. Marshall waited with the rest of them to hear what Vin might say next.

Seconds ticked by before Vincent turned around. He looked at each of them. "I was so adamant that Riley have a normal life. I sent her to Austin for her degree, and I got so caught up with everything that I didn't even realize she'd graduated. She didn't tell us. Or maybe she tried during one of the calls that I cut short because it was too painful to talk to her. But I pushed her away, believing it was the right thing to do. What did that get us? Our sister living in New Orleans, away from us."

"She was with our cousins," Christian said.

Lincoln crossed his arms over his chest. "Who let her hunt."

Beau glared at Linc. "As if you would've been able to stop her. At least our cousins made her hunt with them so they could keep an eye on her."

"She wouldn't have been taken had she been home," Linc stated.

"I'm not so sure of that," Vin said before the argument could continue.

Marshall waited for the brothers to ask what Vin meant, and when they didn't, he finally said the words. "What do you mean?"

"That Delphine wanted to hurt us," Christian said.

Linc nodded. "If the Voodoo bitch wanted Riley, it wouldn't have mattered where she was."

"And by taking her while our cousins were watching over her, it ensured that there would be a rift between our families," Beau finished.

Marshall returned his gaze to Vin. "Then don't let that happen. Everyone respects and fears the LaRues because they don't hesitate to put people in their place. The LaRues run New Orleans. The Chiassons run Lyons Point. Imagine if the two of you joined forces."

"Like Christian said, we can't leave the area," Linc said.

Marshall set his hand on the butt of his gun at his hip. "There has been an increase in activity since Riley was taken, hasn't there?"

Vin's brows drew together. "We rarely get a night off, but now that you mention it, yes. Instead of us hunting one creature a night, we're tracking down multiple, forcing us to split up."

"It's Delphine," Beau said with a shake of his head, a vein ticking in his temple.

"No doubt, but that doesn't help us." Linc looked at Vin and shrugged. "What do we do?"

Vin ran a hand down his face. "What can we do? Save our sister, or keep the parish safe."

"What if I went to New Orleans?" Four pairs of vivid blue eyes turned Marshall's way. He looked at each brother before he locked eyes with Vincent. "I still have a lot of friends in New Orleans. I grew up in the area, and I worked there for seven years, so I know it well. The LaRues have been searching the paranormal world, but perhaps someone needs to take a look at the human one."

Vin walked toward him, stopping a few feet away. "You would do that for us?"

"Like you said, you can't leave. I can. I can put my deputy in charge here. And Delphine won't be looking for me."

Linc shrugged when Vin looked his way. "Marshall has a point."

"I say yes," Christian chimed in.

Beau smiled and clapped Marshall on the shoulder. "There are some things you're going to need."

2

New Orleans

*T*here was something different. Riley could feel it deep within her, but she couldn't put a name to it. She walked the streets, holding a bag in each hand from her run to the grocery store.

The sun felt glorious on her face. If only she didn't have to get back and start cooking, she would climb on top of the roof of the house in her bathing suit and catch some rays. After so many days of rain, she didn't want to pass up the opportunity.

She blinked through her sunglasses at the people passing her. The sight of two brothers good-naturedly teasing their younger sister made her stop and stare. There was something about the siblings that stirred an emotion within her, a feeling she couldn't quite name.

"Something wrong?"

She jerked her head around to find Delphine beside her. Riley smiled in welcome. "I was just watching the kids."

"You should've brought George with you," Delphine said. "He could've helped with the bags."

Riley rolled her eyes as she shook her head. "I'm more than capable of carrying them. George doesn't need to follow me everywhere. Besides, I've been doing really good this week."

"So you have."

Riley stood still so Delphine could inspect her with her black eyes that seemed to see through everything. She noted that Delphine had once more covered her long, black hair with a white cloth piled high atop her head.

Riley was quite envious of Delphine's mocha skin and seemingly ageless face. But how could she remain jealous of a woman who had taken her in and given her shelter while healing her?

"Come, child," the Voodoo priestess urged.

Riley didn't give the siblings another thought as she walked beside Delphine back to the streets that she ruled. The area was the only place Riley felt safe, so she didn't venture outside of the ten-block radius.

Because, outside of Delphine's domain, lurked the monsters who had attacked her.

"Any headaches today?" Delphine asked.

Riley shrugged. "Minor. I can handle it."

"And the nightmares?"

"None." Riley wasn't sure why she lied. The word was out of her mouth before she realized it, and she couldn't take it back.

Delphine smiled, showing even, white teeth. "That's wonderful news."

"I told you. I'm getting better."

"Yes, you are, my dear."

Riley preened when Delphine put an arm around her. Everyone they passed stared in awe because every one of them wanted to be in Riley's place. She was well aware how lucky she was to have Delphine take her in. Why the priestess had chosen her when there were thousands of others she could've picked, Riley would never know. But she would never turn on Delphine.

Once they reached the house, Riley made her way to the kitchen, looking for her friend, Elin, as she did. She couldn't remember ever having trained to cook—or even where she learned—but she was decent at it. And she liked the activity. It was her way of repaying Delphine for everything.

She set the bags of groceries on the table and took each item out before putting them away. Then she got out a knife and sharpened it before peeling and chopping the garlic and onions.

Riley turned on the radio and smiled when an Eagles song came on. She continued the prep for the spicy shrimp fettuccine while she sang. She didn't know how long she stood there before she felt as if someone were watching.

A glance over her shoulder confirmed that someone was. She flashed a quick smile at the young man who had deemed himself her protector while trying not to shiver in dread. George was nice, but there was just something about him that set her on edge.

"Delphine said you went out alone," George said as he ran a hand over his short, black hair.

Riley rinsed the knife and nodded, not looking into George's black eyes. "I needed to do it. Besides, it was a quick trip. And I was fine."

"No one bothered you?"

She laughed and set the knife down as she faced him. "The only person who spoke to me was the cashier. It was actually good. I feel good, too."

He moved closer, his eyes searching her face. She wasn't able to back up, and while he had a nice body and an attractive face with his deep black skin, he made her uncomfortable.

"I can see that," he said.

"I'm getting better."

"It's only been a couple of months. You should take it slow."

She glanced away. He'd made it known that he was interested in taking their relationship further, but she didn't have those types of feelings for him. The fact that she'd leaned on him for so long allowed him to think they were getting closer like that. It was one of the reasons she'd gone to the store by herself.

"I am taking it slow," Riley said before turning back to the food.

But he didn't take the hint. George drew closer as he came up behind her. "I worry about you. The way I found you that night—"

"I know," she said before he could continue the sentence.

He tenderly spun her around. "That's just it. You don't. You didn't see what I saw."

"You explained it to me." She sidestepped to put some distance between them. "I don't want to talk about that night again. I want to put it in the past."

His face fell as his hands dropped to his sides. "Put it in the past then, but don't ever forget it."

She didn't move until he turned and walked out of the kitchen. Only then did she resume the prep. Riley turned up the music and immersed herself in the meal creation to drown out the thoughts that were growing louder in her mind.

If she were lucky, she'd get some time alone with Elin to share her feelings. It seemed Riley wasn't the only one Delphine saved from an attack. Elin had also been brought to the house to recover. Riley was thankful for her friend, because Elin had been a comfort during all the horrible recovery days.

Riley loved the moon. She could stare at it all night, just as she did now. Every evening, she sat beside her window on the second floor and gazed up at the orb. It didn't seem to bother Delphine that Riley wasn't part of the Voodoo religion. If

Delphine asked, Riley would have gladly joined in, but the priestess had never pushed.

Muted music reached her. Apparently, there was another gathering of Delphine and her followers. The drums beat a rhythm that was both steady and sensual.

Movement below her caught Riley's attention. She saw George walking in a pair of white linen pants that billowed around his legs. His muscular chest was bare, and his chocolate skin gleamed in the moonlight. He paused and looked up at her before continuing on.

Curious, Riley rose and hurried down the stairs to the back entrance of the large manor. The family next door had given their home to Delphine to use for her gatherings. For long minutes, Riley stood in the entryway, looking across the lawn. Finally, she took a step out and closed the door behind her. She walked barefoot toward the house, the beating of the drums seeming to match her pounding heart.

The music held her in thrall. The concrete was still warm from the sun, but the grass was cool upon her feet. She walked toward the open door where she saw a red-orange glow from the many candles within the dwelling.

She reached the entrance, but hesitated. There was something about the house that seemed familiar, which couldn't be right. She'd never been inside it before.

The music subtly shifted. Her eyes wouldn't stay focused, and her limbs grew heavy. And through it all, something drew her forward, into the building.

Someone touched her. It took a great amount of effort for her to turn her head and see that one of Delphine's followers had taken her arm. The older woman was chanting something as she guided Riley.

Soon, someone was on her other side. She couldn't tell them no, couldn't refuse them. Nor could she yank herself away. She was powerless, but she wasn't scared. In fact, she was calm.

And that worried her.

Something in her mind shouted for her to run, to get far away.

Suddenly, Riley was on her knees in the middle of the room. Delphine came to stand before her with her arms raised upward. Riley tried to keep her eyes open as people gathered around them in a circle, their chants strident—but not as loud as the music.

Riley realized it held her captive. There was something in the notes, some rhythm or melody that made her a slave.

Delphine put her hand atop Riley's head as she shouted something. Riley's arms were taken once more and held out at her sides. Someone came up behind her, pressing against her. Then they were gone.

Riley could feel sleep calling to her, but she fought it. She wanted to know what was going on. And she needed to know who was touching her. It had been nothing sexual…yet. But she could sense the carnal, wanton atmosphere within the room.

It took several tries before she was able to open her eyes. The women holding her were rocking, causing her to sway upon her knees. Delphine released Riley's head and took three steps back, her eyes closed the entire time.

Riley couldn't understand the words of Delphine's chant, but she felt their power. Hell, she could feel the magic within the room. It pulsed, growing with each beat of the drums.

No longer could she keep her eyes open. She let them fall shut, listening to the music and the murmur of the people around her. She didn't know how long she remained that way before the women released her arms and slowly laid her on the floor. Though Riley fought the blackness that threatened to claim her, it was too strong. She was lulled to sleep by the sensual tune.

Somehow, she clawed her way back to consciousness. The music still filled the room, but it was...different. Riley slit open a lid and saw that the group around her was gone.

Yet she wasn't alone. She could hear heavy breathing and soft moans. Without having to see, Riley knew someone was having sex. She wanted to leave, but her body wouldn't obey. It was as if it belonged to someone else.

She opened her eyes further and caught sight of a foot. She followed it up until she saw George lying naked on his back with Delphine atop him, writhing in lust—all while George's eyes were on *her*.

Delphine looked over at her and grinned. Then she leaned over George and stroked his face. "Soon," she whispered.

Riley could only watch as Delphine rose and walked toward her, her breasts jiggling with each step. Riley noticed the priestess was clean-shaven between her legs.

Delphine kneeled beside Riley and stroked her hair before moving her hand along Riley's cheek and then down to her breast. Riley tried to tense, but once more, her body denied her control.

"Shhh," the priestess said in a low tone. "Stop fighting this. We won't hurt you. We're protecting you. Remember? We saved you. We're making you stronger."

Safe. Yes, Riley knew she was safe and protected with Delphine.

"Yes. That's it," the priestess said. "Let my magic work to finish healing you. It called to you tonight, and you answered. That means there is something special in store for you." Delphine leaned closer after glancing at George. "And you have a man who longs to have you as his own."

Riley tried to shake her head.

"Shhhhhhhhh," Delphine insisted. "Not tonight. Tonight, he's mine. But soon, my dear, you'll want him as much as he wants you. Think of the beautiful babies the two of you will make. Dark and light together."

Delphine let her hand continue down Riley's side as the music grew louder. The last thing Riley saw before sleep claimed her again was Delphine taking George within her body once more.

3

There was something about the city of New Orleans that set it apart from anywhere else in the world. There were those who believed it was the people that made it stand out. And that was true.

In a sense.

Marshall drove down Charles Street in the heart of the French Quarter, looking at the people—and the supernatural beings. Because it was the mystical aspects that made New Orleans a mecca, boasting the largest concentration of such individuals on the continent.

He meandered through the streets until he came to Gator Bait. The bar owned by the LaRues was a favorite of both locals and tourists, but Marshall didn't stop. For now, he was going to search for Riley on his own. He knew without a doubt that he'd eventually have to come to the LaRues, but not until he had no other choice.

For the next hour, he drove all over New Orleans until the sun went down. He made a stop at a local store to pick up some food. Then Marshall pulled into the driveway of his old partner's house and turned off the ignition. He sat in his truck for a moment before he grabbed his duffle bag and headed to the front porch.

Marshall was glad that Donnie was out of town for the next week on a cruise with his girlfriend. It would allow Marshall to go about his business without having to hide anything from his friend.

Inside the house, he made his way to the spare bedroom and dropped his bag on the bed. He unzipped it and pulled out the files of everything he had on Riley. Then, he walked to the kitchen and laid it all out on the table.

Marshall got out a steak and seasoned it while reading over everywhere the LaRues and Chiassons had looked for Riley. Like the rest of them, Marshall was sure she was still somewhere in the city.

The problem was the city itself. There were so many places for her to be hidden away, especially the area that Delphine had claimed as hers. The Chiassons hadn't ventured into that district, not that he blamed them. They'd gotten as close as they could, but their clashes with the priestess made them targets. The four LaRue brothers, as guardians of the city, were able to freely walk the streets, but they'd gleaned nothing that could help either. Marshall hoped he would have better luck.

He went out back and lit the gas grill before returning to the kitchen to open a can of baked beans. In no time, he was sitting at the table eating his steak and beans and studying the map of New Orleans.

Without a doubt, the first place he needed to look was in Delphine's district. He'd agreed to contact the Chiassons twice a day, every day, with his location. If he didn't, they would assume that something happened to him and would know where to begin searching.

He'd been a damn good detective with the NOPD. He loved the city, but he didn't love how the supernatural had important and influential people of the community in their pockets. Those high-ranking individuals—including his superior—had made Marshall repeatedly let guilty parties go because they happened to be supernaturals.

The only sect who hadn't given the NOPD any shit were the werewolves. Mostly because the LaRues were the only ones around back then, but that was changing with the reemergence of the Moonstone pack.

After his meal was finished, Marshall sent a quick text to the Chiassons, letting them know he was at the house and settling in for the night. Then he began to go over the different factions within the city to mark off who wasn't involved with Riley's disappearance.

Obviously, the weres weren't involved. The LaRues would've sniffed out if someone from another pack had taken their cousin, so that faction was quickly scratched off.

The vampires could have done it, but it wasn't likely. They liked to make a statement, so if they had been the ones to abduct Riley, they would've either turned her or killed her—and either way, they would've shown her off to the LaRues afterward.

The djinn were a possibility. They certainly had the power to do it, and their victims weren't usually recovered. Though they generally kept to themselves, they had been consorting with vampires recently. Still, if a djinn had Riley, a vamp would've found out and quickly told everyone, thinking it would give them an advantage over the LaRues.

As for the witches, they had no reason to want to harm Riley, the LaRues, or the Chiassons since it was one of their own, Minka, who'd stood up to Delphine recently. And the LaRues had helped to band the witches together as they all stood and fought the priestess.

So that only left Delphine.

It was the same conclusion the LaRues and Chiassons had

come to. And it meant that Marshall would have to tread carefully.

He'd seen Delphine when she came to Lyons Point to try and get Davena to join her followers. The sheer amount of power the priestess possessed terrified Marshall because he had nothing to combat it. Not his gun or his knife could damage Delphine.

But she could do a number of things to him with just a thought.

That wasn't going to stop him from searching for Riley, though. It had been over eight weeks since she was last seen. That was eight weeks of suffering at Delphine's hand. Just as Marshall was sure Riley was in the Voodoo district, he was sure she was alive. If Delphine had wanted her dead, she could've killed Riley on the street.

No, the priestess had something else in mind for Riley, a plan that would strike at both the LaRues' and Chiassons' jugulars. The question was: what? What could she possibly do that would stop two such strong families from coming for her?

Because it would happen. It was simply a matter of when. Right now, they were waiting to locate Riley. Once that was done, the two families would unite and descend upon Delphine and her followers.

All that was holding them back was Riley.

Marshall shook his head as a thought took root. It was a dangerous one, and something that left him a bit sick to his stomach. He rose and went to the fridge for another lager. He twisted the cap and lifted the longneck bottle to his lips to drink deeply.

He set the beer down on the counter and braced his hands on either side of it, hanging his head.

"Fuck me," he murmured.

Riley's brothers and cousins were so wrapped up in locating

her while praying she was alive, that none of them had stepped back to try and determine what Delphine wanted with Riley.

And Marshall wasn't so sure he wanted to tell anyone his theory just yet. Because if he was right, and the Chiassons and LaRues learned that Delphine was using Riley as a shield of sorts, that would keep both families from ever attacking. Marshall wasn't sure what they would do.

He ran a hand down his face and straightened. Damn. His job had just gotten harder, not that it had been easy to begin with. If his prediction were correct, then Delphine would be watching anyone in her district closely—especially outsiders.

She'd need a place to keep Riley so that she couldn't escape, but also someplace that Delphine could show the Chiassons and LaRues to get them to back off.

Marshall didn't know the Voodoo area as well as he knew some of the other parishes. He hadn't been stationed there while still in uniform, and once he'd made detective, the police were rarely called into that area.

He grabbed a cupcake that he'd bought and walked back to the table. Once back in his seat, he studied the map again, memorizing the streets of Delphine's area as he ate the sweet. Between the map and looking at various pictures of Riley that all the Chiassons had sent to his phone, he was at the table for hours.

At midnight, he stretched his back and rose to walk around. His feet took him to the front door. He opened it and looked out the screen to the world beyond. A full moon was coming, and that meant the LaRues would be on full patrol because things really went crazy in the city during that time.

The night air was cool, the crickets and frogs noisy between the sounds of the passing cars. But it was the creatures beyond that he was concerned with.

He'd been given all sorts of weapons to fight with. They were in his truck, but now he wished he would've brought them in. Though, honestly, this was probably the only night he could sleep without them.

Once his search began, he would have to place them all over the house, on his person, and even in various places in his truck so a weapon was always near. Imagine, at one time, he'd believed the worst thing he would ever track down was a serial killer who had murdered six blond college girls.

That was eight years ago, when the monsters he protected innocents from were both human and supernatural alike.

His phone rang behind him. Marshall shut and locked the door before going to answer it. "Hello?"

"Hey," Christian said. "Everything good?"

"Yep. Didn't you get my text?"

There was a bit of a hesitation. "I did. I was hoping for more information."

Marshall smiled because he'd been expecting this from one of the brothers—if not all of them. "I don't know anything yet. I just got here, remember?"

"Yeah, I know. I just...well, shit. The thing is, I wish I was with you."

"There's a part of me that wishes you were here, as well. But it'll be better if I search on my own."

Christian released a long sigh. "Give me something, man. I'm going crazy over here."

"I drove around all over, even in Delphine's area, but I didn't see anything."

"Yeah," Christian replied in a desolate voice.

Marshall stared at the map. "I'm going to do everything I can to find her."

"I know you will, but she's not your sister."

"No, but that's not going to stop me. She's your sister, and you and your brothers are my friends."

Christian said, "You're a good man and a good friend, but I'm worried—"

"That I'm out of my element?" he finished.

That made Christian chuckle. "Well, yeah."

"No one is more aware of that fact than I am. I might have helped y'all out a few times, but that's much different than being on my own. And it's Delphine."

"She scares the shit out of everyone, including me."

Marshall grinned. "That's saying something."

"If you knew something, or figured something out, you'd tell me, right?"

"Of course," he lied. There was no need to get Christian and his brothers riled up before Marshall had more information.

Christian cleared his throat. "I know. I'm sorry. I just had to ask."

"None of you have told the LaRues I'm here, have you?"

"Give us some credit, man. You've only been gone twelve hours."

Marshall rolled his eyes. "Who wanted to call them?"

"It might have been me."

"Dude."

"I know, I know. I'm just worried you're going to step into something you can't handle."

Marshall made a sound in the back of his throat. "For fuck's sake. You do know I was a cop in New Orleans for seven years, right? And I was a Marine."

"Yeah."

"I survived that just fine."

Christian let a lengthy pause grow before he said, "But you didn't have Delphine to worry about."

For some reason, Riley couldn't stop staring at the house next to Delphine's. It was smaller and uninhabited and didn't look the least bit inviting. But that had nothing to do with the look of the house.

It was clean, and the yard was maintained, but for the life of her, Riley didn't like the building. And the longer she stood out in the sun and stared at it, the more she disliked it.

"Riley?"

She jumped at the sound of George's voice behind her. Riley grabbed her throat and forced a laugh when she turned to him. "Oh, hey, you scared me."

"I'm sorry," he said with a soft smile. "What are you looking at?"

Her gaze shot to the house before she quickly looked away. "What do you know about the people who used to live there?"

"Nothing much. They had to move away, and they signed the house over to Delphine."

There was the briefest moment where Riley thought she knew that, but it vanished as quickly as it had appeared. "Does Delphine use it?"

"Occasionally. Why are you asking?"

"I don't know."

His brow furrowed as he stepped closer to her. "You had another migraine last night, didn't you?"

She couldn't remember much of the evening before, and that usually signaled that it had been a migraine. Thank God she had someone like Delphine to look out for her. "I think so."

"You shouldn't overdo it today," he advised.

"I appreciate your concern, but I'm fine."

She moved past him and walked back into the house through the back door that brought her immediately into the kitchen. When the door didn't shut directly behind her, she knew George had followed her.

"Riley," he began.

Grabbing her shopping list, she turned to face him. "Please, don't. I'm fine."

"I'm concerned about you."

"Because Delphine told you to be?" She had no idea where that thought had come from or why it even left her lips.

Hurt cut across his handsome features. "No. Because I care about you."

"Because you found me that horrible night eight weeks ago. You feel responsible."

He gave a shake of his head. "That's not it at all."

"I went to the store yesterday by myself, and it was amazing. I need to be able to do things on my own again. So, I'm going to walk out the door and do as I did before. I'm even going to take a little more time today."

His brows snapped together. "I don't think that's a good idea."

She rolled her eyes and shoved her hair away from her face. "I'm not a prisoner. Delphine said I could come and go as I please."

George took a step back. His hands clenched, and his frown deepened while his gaze dropped to the floor as if he were searching for something to say to change her mind.

But there wasn't anything that would alter the course she had set for herself. She might not remember much of her past, but she knew she had been independent, and she was going to get back to that.

"I'll return soon," she said and looped her purse strap over her shoulder before she headed out the door.

Her steps were quick and light as she bounded down the porch stairs and then over the path to the sidewalk. This time, she left the sunglasses off, even though she had to squint against the sun.

The rays felt too good on her face.

Unable to help herself, she looked at everyone she passed, trying to discern if they had been the ones responsible for her attack. Yet she knew those responsible wouldn't be in this part of the city—because they feared Delphine.

Just as she had told George, Riley took her time, leisurely strolling along the concrete and taking in the glorious city. The plants had begun blooming weeks ago when the weather warmed. She'd missed that, and it was usually one of her favorite things.

That thought made her halt. Every once in a while, a thought like that popped into her mind. She didn't know why it felt as if it had been buried, but now, at the surface, she knew it for a fact.

Moreover, she knew she loved plants. She loved planting and cultivating them. Her favorites were hibiscus, snapdragons, and daisies.

Recalling more of her past that had been taken from her the night of the attack was another sign that she was growing stronger. If only the migraines would stop, because each time they came, she lost time. Sometimes, small bits. Sometimes, hours.

Riley began walking again until she spotted a bench near a street performer. The sound of the violin was a call she couldn't ignore. Somewhere, sometime, she had gone to a symphony and enjoyed it.

She sat on the bench and closed her eyes while the rays of the sun bathed her face, and the music filled her ears. The soft melody drowned out the sounds of conversations around her as well as the cars.

Several songs were played before she finally opened her eyes. Just as she was about to get up, her gaze landed on a dark-headed man off to her left. His wavy hair was just a bit on the longish side, enough that he shoved it out of his face with his hand.

He was lean and rugged, his skin bronzed by the sun. His gaze was locked on the woman playing the violin, his toe tapping along with the music. He wore a simple navy V-neck tee that stretched across his wide shoulders and around his defined arms. Faded denim hugged his trim hips.

While his body was certainly nice, it was his face that she found herself staring at. His cheekbones, jaw, and chin were cut with chiseled perfection. And the slight shadow of a beard only made him sexier. Yet his wide lips were slightly turned up at the corners, softening his look.

Suddenly, his head turned slightly, their gazes clashing. She was mesmerized by his beautiful silver eyes. Maybe that's why she saw the slight widening of his gaze as if he recognized her.

But he didn't approach her right away. Instead, he turned back to the performer. When she finished her set, he walked to her and dug out some money from his wallet before tossing it into her opened violin case.

Riley sat up straighter when the man then turned her way.

She wanted him to come talk to her. For someone who was so terrified of her own shadow a few weeks earlier, she was making great headway now.

He smiled and gave her a nod as he approached. "Hello."

"Hi," she replied. "The violinist was quite good."

He glanced over his shoulder. "That she was."

"Are you from New Orleans?"

"I grew up close to the city, and I've worked here for some time. You?"

She was shocked when the answer came out of nowhere—again. "I've only been here a short while. I'm Riley, by the way. Riley Chiasson."

"Marshall Ducet," he said and held out his hand.

Riley couldn't stop smiling when she shook his hand. Reluctantly, she released him, suddenly at a loss for words.

"What brought you to the city?" he asked.

She looked away as her mind shut down. "I don't remember."

"Did something happen to you?"

It was the concern in his voice that drew her gaze back to him. He looked at her as if all he cared about was her. It warmed her heart in ways she couldn't explain. And there, just for a millisecond, she thought she knew him. "Yes, something happened."

"Are you okay now?"

She didn't know why she felt so at ease with him, but she did. "I am. I'm sorry, but have we met before?"

"No."

There was some emotion in his gray eyes, almost as if he were holding something back. "There was an attack. I hit my head, and I lost some of my memory."

"An attack?"

Two words. That's all it took for the grin to vanish and his gaze to turn hard in anger *for* her.

"What happened?" he demanded in a soft voice.

Normally, she didn't like to talk about it, but she found herself wanting to share with him. But she hesitated.

His dark brows drew together. "What's wrong?"

"I can't explain it or my reaction to you."

He blinked and sat beside her. "I think I'm confused."

She gave a shake of her head. "That's my fault, I apologize. I don't usually like to talk about the attack, but there's something about you that I innately trust, something that makes me want to tell you."

"And that frightens you?"

"A little," she confessed. "It could have been that same trust that caused the attack in the first place."

His lips thinned for a moment. "I doubt that."

"You sound sure of yourself."

"I work in law enforcement. I've seen and heard about all sorts of attacks, and trusting your gut isn't ever the cause of one."

She blew out a breath. "Maybe."

"You don't have to tell me if you don't want to. I just couldn't imagine anyone wanting to harm you."

She smiled, liking him more and more. "If I tell you the truth, you might think I'm crazy."

"Never," he said and leaned back. He turned his head to her. "If you want to talk, I'll gladly listen."

"Are you married?" She had no idea why that was important, but she had to know the answer.

He chuckled softly. "No. I've never been married. You?"

"No." Of that, she was sure. Just like she'd known she liked flowers.

"Good."

Yes, it was good. Riley held Marshall's gaze and said, "There are supernatural creatures in New Orleans."

"I know."

His casual response was all she needed to continue. "I was out walking one night when I was viciously attacked by a werewolf. It was trying to kill me, and in the struggle, I slammed my head on the pavement. My friend, Delphine, heard my screams and came to rescue me. She brought me to her house and has given me shelter as I healed."

"Delphine?" he asked in a voice devoid of any inflection.

But his eyes said it all. He didn't like the priestess.

"You know her?" Riley asked.

He lifted one shoulder in a shrug as he looked away. "Everyone who knows about the paranormal knows of Delphine."

"And you don't like her."

Silver eyes returned to her. "I didn't say that."

"You didn't have to. It's in your gaze."

He glanced down before shifting to face her. "I'm glad she helped you."

"I've known nothing but kindness from her. Nothing bad can get to me in her district."

He smiled, but it didn't quite reach his eyes. "So you don't need to worry about werewolves."

"Exactly."

Marshall ran a hand over his mouth, a frown forming. "I'm sorry for what happened to you, Riley. I imagine your family has been worried about you."

"I don't have family."

"No one?" he pressed.

She shook her head. "It's why I'm so blessed to have Delphine in my life."

"Indeed."

Riley looked at her watch. "Shit. I need to go, but I've enjoyed talking to you. I'm sorry I can't stay."

"Meet me here tomorrow."

Her heart nearly erupted in joy. "I'd like that. Until then, Marshall Ducet."

"Stay safe, Riley Chiasson."

She rose and walked away. After a few steps, she looked back over her shoulder to find him watching her. He waved, causing her stomach to flutter in excitement.

5

*M*arshall sat at the kitchen table with his elbows on his knees as he stared at his cell phone. Though he'd promised to call the Chiassons and update them, he knew he couldn't tell them anything.

He kept going over his accidental meeting with Riley in his head. While only seeing her once before—briefly—and staring at her photos on his phone, her image was branded in his mind.

It's why he'd recognized her instantly.

To think, he had almost turned down the previous street, but the performer had sounded so good that he needed a closer look.

As soon as his gaze clashed with her bright blue eyes, Marshall had known it was Riley. The fact that she had sat there as if she didn't have a care in the world is what tightened the ball of worry in his stomach.

It was why he hadn't gone to her right away. He'd needed time to gather his thoughts on how to approach her. But it was nearly impossible not to look at the Cajun beauty.

Luxurious dark hair tumbled down her back in soft waves. She'd had one side tucked behind her ear, showing off her long, slender throat. Her wide, slightly angled eyes looked at every-thing as if seeing it all for the first time.

With her high cheekbones, simple beauty, and lips so full and sinful that he ached to touch them, Riley had people of all ages looking her way. And she seemed completely unaware of her allure, which made her even more attractive.

He'd approached her cautiously, not entirely sure what to say. Yet, she'd smiled in welcome, though there hadn't been any recognition in her eyes. Why would there be? They had never actually met. The one time she'd seen him, she was leaving to return to New Orleans and her cousins. Her thoughts had been on anything but him.

The fact that she thought she was with Delphine because of a werewolf attack made Marshall sick to his stomach. Just as he'd guessed, Delphine planned to use Riley against her family. He just hadn't expected the Voodoo priestess's actions to be quite so sinister.

To take away the one thing the Chiassons cared about above all else, all while making Riley believe she had no family. And ensure that the LaRues could never convince Riley to return to them.

Marshall hung his head and blew out a long breath. Obvi-ously, Delphine believed in her magic enough to allow Riley off on her own. Then again, Riley believed every word she said. The conviction had been in her voice and her actions.

Where exactly did that leave Marshall? It wasn't like he could tell Riley the truth. She wouldn't believe him, and then he might lose the only chance he had of getting her away from Delphine.

But how did he convince Riley of what was really going on?

His phone rang. Marshall lifted his head and pursed his lips when he saw the Caller ID. He lifted the phone to his ear and said, "Hey, Vin."

"Hey. I wanted to see how things were progressing."

Marshall closed his eyes as he sat back in the chair. He heard the anxiety and worry in Vincent's voice, and he could only imagine how the eldest Chiasson was handling things.

"Slow."

"I'm going insane here, Marshall. My siblings are my responsibility. If anything happens to Riley—"

"It's not going to," Marshall interjected. "Don't go down that road. You need to stay positive for your brothers."

Vin sighed loudly. "Where did you look today?"

"Look, I know you're worried, and I know you want to be here searching yourself, but perhaps it's better if you don't second-guess everything I'm doing."

Besides, Marshall didn't like lying to his friends, and with every call where he didn't tell them about Riley, it would eat at him.

"Shit. That's not what I'm doing," Vin said. "I'm sorry. I just want something to hold on to, something that says my sister is going to come back to us."

Marshall tilted his head back to look at the ceiling. "We all know how strong Delphine is. Her magic is powerful."

"Davena was telling us all the different ways Delphine could hurt Riley. I had to ask the question, which made Davena answer it. That Voodoo bitch wants to destroy our family, Marshall. And she's going to use Riley to do it."

"I know."

Vincent snorted. "Christian said you'd probably figured that out."

"It makes the most sense."

"Well, at least my sister is alive."

Marshall closed his eyes. "Yeah."

"You shouldn't be there, and you especially shouldn't be going up against Delphine alone. This family has lost a lot of friends over the years. We don't want to lose you, as well."

"Since I'm not ready to kick the bucket just yet, I'm treading carefully."

Vincent was silent for a moment. "Be safe, Marshall. And don't trust anyone."

Don't trust anyone.

Vincent's words rang in Marshall's head the next day as he waited on the bench for Riley. Though Vin hadn't said it, he was telling Marshall to be wary of Riley if he encountered her.

And after his brief conversation with the youngest Chiasson the previous day, Marshall planned to take everything she said with a grain of salt.

He glanced at his watch. It was thirty-seven minutes past the time Riley was supposed to meet him. Since everything hinged on their speaking again, he didn't intend to leave. He'd stay there all damn day if he had to.

At least the violinist was back. Marshall spread his arms along the back of the bench and stretched out his legs, one ankle crossed over the other.

The detective in him took in everything around him, cataloging it in his mind—because details were important. He noted the people walking past him, the ones listening to the performer, and those who milled about for other reasons. It was easy for him to spot and separate the tourists from those who lived in the city.

In many ways, he missed the vibrant hum of New Orleans, the mix of the old and new, and how it seemed to seamlessly mesh together. Fun and danger mingled together like dance partners, each trying to take the lead.

And thrown into the jumble was the supernatural.

Someone approaching on his right caused Marshall to turn

his head in that direction. The concern that had been courting him each minute Riley was late vanished when he saw her.

"I can't believe you're still here," she said with a relieved smile as she stopped beside the bench.

Marshall motioned for her to sit beside him. He looked over Riley's gray jeans and white shirt, appreciating how both garments showed off her body. "I had nowhere else I wanted to be."

She pushed her hair back over her shoulder and turned so that she faced him. "I'm sorry for being late. I couldn't get away."

"Everything all right now?" he asked as he covertly looked around for anyone who might be following her.

It didn't take long for Marshall to find the tall, black man who stared at Riley as if she were his favorite toy, one that had been stolen by someone else.

Riley laughed softly and leaned back. "Yes. I'm glad you waited."

They stared at each other for a few minutes before she looked away. Finally, she asked, "How do you know about the supernatural?"

"You can't be a cop in this city and not see something. I also know people who hunt the evil creatures."

Her head cocked to the side as a small frown puckered her brow. "You make it sound as if there are monsters who are good."

"Would it shock you to know that I know for a fact that some are? Just as humans are both, the same is true for the supernatural."

She looked forward, lines of thought bracketing her mouth. "I always assumed they were all evil."

"Always as in forever, or since the attack?"

Blue eyes slid back to him. "I can't recall what I thought about them before the attack."

"Does that mean that you knew of the supernatural before?"

"Yes," she answered immediately. Then she frowned.

He shifted his body some to face her. "What's wrong?"

"Sometimes, I can answer things like that without knowing how the information is there."

"It's locked in your mind."

A grin curved her luscious lips. "You make it sound as if my memories have been secured away."

"In a way, they have." The longer the tall man stared at Riley, the angrier Marshall became. "How long do I have with you?"

"As long as you want."

"Is that so?" he asked with a grin. Then he got to his feet and held out his hand. "Do you trust me?"

She took his hand and stood. "Yes, though I don't know why."

Marshall wrapped his fingers around hers. "Let's walk."

They talked of easy things like the weather and tourists. Riley laughed and joked right up until they reached the edge of Delphine's domain where she came to a halt. Marshall said nothing as he watched Riley, whose gaze was glued to the invisible line before her. On the surface, she looked calm, but he noticed that her breathing had quickened, and her fingers now gripped his hand tightly.

"If I leave this section of the city, the supernatural can get to me."

He turned her to face him. "I don't want to scare you, but the fact is, the monsters can get you anywhere—even in this part of the city."

"No. Delphine wouldn't allow that."

"I'm sure she wouldn't," he answered. There was no need to try and persuade her differently.

Riley licked her lips and glanced at the ground where the invisible marker was that sectioned off Delphine's part of the city. "I don't like living in fear. The longer I hide from it, the longer it's going to take me to get my life back."

"We can turn around," he offered.

She looked at him and lifted her chin. "No. We're going forward."

"Lead the way, Miss Chiasson."

Riley was smiling—and still holding his hand—when she stepped over the boundary into the vampire sector of the city.

They walked quietly for some time before she glanced at him. "You look at me as if you know me."

"What would you say if I said I did?"

She shrugged and shifted to allow another couple to pass on the sidewalk. "I'd want to know from where and how."

As they passed a restaurant, Marshall looked in the windows and saw the black man's reflection from across the street. No matter where they went, he was going to follow them. And Marshall wanted Riley alone.

He looked down at her lips, his balls tightening.

Oh how he wanted that kiss.

"How do you feel about boat rides?"

Her eyes grew large as she grinned. "I love the water."

"Good," he replied.

In a matter of moments, they were at the water's edge, where they jumped on one of the tour boats. Marshall inwardly smiled when the vessel pushed away from the pier with no other passengers getting on behind them.

He and Riley walked to the opposite side of the boat to the railing. Someone bumped into her from behind, sending her straight into his arms.

Marshall held her protectively as he gazed down into her eyes. God, how he wanted to taste her lips.

6

*G*od, how she wanted to kiss him. Riley's palms were flattened against Marshall's chest, and she could feel the heat and hardness of his sinew through the black shirt. Desire scorched her, leaving a trail of need in its wake.

The way his gunmetal eyes looked at her, truly seeing her as a person and not an object, made her skin tingle. She enjoyed being in his arms and feeling his strength. He walked and looked like a man who could take on anything, and she felt safe with him.

Before she could think about it, she rose up and pressed her lips briefly to his. As she was drawing back, he captured her mouth and slid his tongue along her lip. Riley opened for him immediately.

The taste of him was heady, intoxicating, and caused her body to warm, and longing to quicken her blood.

He kissed her slowly, thoroughly. Gradually deepening the kiss until she was clinging to him, need thrumming through her as her sex ached. His arms were the only reason she was still on her feet.

When he ended the kiss and looked down at her, she struggled to get herself under control, fought not to pull his head down for another taste of his amazing lips. Because, damn, the man could kiss.

"I've been wanting to do that for a long time," he said in a low, soft voice.

"Then why in the hell did you stop?"

He smoothed hair away from her face. "I didn't want to. In fact, I don't ever want to stop."

Something was happening between them. Desire, yes, but something more primal, more untamed swirled between them. Though it frightened her a little, she didn't want it to end. Ever. It felt so good, like basking in the glow of the sun.

Whoever Marshall Ducet was, she knew she could trust him, and that he would keep her safe. She didn't question that—or the craving she had for him.

His hand splayed on her back, pulling her against him so she felt his arousal. Her stomach fluttered, and desire pooled low in her belly. She lifted her face, silently begging for him to kiss her again.

"I can hardly think with you near," he murmured.

"Stop thinking."

His eyes darkened as he stared at her, his craving blatant. And palpable.

Breathing became impossible as she struggled not to tear his clothes off. The crush of people was a constant reminder that they weren't alone.

His other hand came up along her side, his thumb stopping at the base of her breast. He held it there, teasing her while he leaned forward and brushed his lips along her throat. Her moan was drowned out by the person speaking through the speakers while pointing out sights. Marshall's hot mouth made a trail from her neck to her ear.

"I want you," he whispered.

She took his head in her hands and moved it so that he was looking at her. "Yes," she said just before pulling him down for another kiss.

The rest of the world fell away, leaving only the two of them and the raging, rampant desire that burned uncontrollably between them. He felt so good, so right. Like they had been destined to meet. Now, all she had to worry about were her brothers.

She jerked back, breaking the kiss as she searched her mind to continue the thought. The thread she clung to evaporated, taking the certainty of family with it. She didn't have any brothers. She was alone in the world.

Then what happened to your family?

"Riley?" Marshall asked as he studied her, worry in his slate-gray gaze.

She swallowed and shook her head, facing the railing to look over the water. "I'm sorry. I just...I...."

"Shhh," he said and put an arm around her. "It's all right."

She stood there, waiting for him to press for more. When he didn't, she looked over at him. "This is normally the part where people ask what's going through my mind."

He pulled his gaze from the water and shot her a half smile before raking a hand through his dark locks. "Something traumatic happened to you. Your mind is trying to work it all out. The less you worry about giving answers, the quicker they'll come to you."

"Is that your professional opinion?" she teased.

A soft chuckle fell from his lips. "Actually, yes. I've seen a lot of horrible things working in law enforcement. There are times to push someone for answers, and there are times when we can tell that a person just needs some space. Right now, you need someone to stand with you while you sort through everything."

"Have you had much experience with head trauma?"

There was a slight pause before he turned to her, leaning his other arm on the railing while still touching her. "How do you know you had head trauma? Did you go to a hospital? Did a doctor see you?"

With every question, she found herself frowning. "I... No. Delphine found me and took care of me."

"Do you remember the attack?"

"Bits and pieces," she said with a shrug.

He nodded slowly. "Then how do you know what happened?"

"George told me how he found me."

"George, huh?"

The wind coming off the water was cooling her heated skin. "George is one of Delphine's followers."

"I thought Delphine found you."

"She did."

"But you just said George found you."

Riley rubbed her temple. "He did."

"Were they together?"

"I don't know," she snapped. Then she took a deep breath. "I'm sorry."

Marshall rubbed his hand along her back. "No, I'm sorry. I shouldn't have pushed you. Old habits, and all that."

She gave him a quick smile. "The thing is, your questions have merit. They made me revisit what I've been told, and I can't answer your last question. Mainly because I'm not sure if they were together or not. Neither has said they were with anyone."

"Will you tell me about the attack when you're ready?"

Riley scooted closer to Marshall and looked back out over the water, shaking her head to loosen the strands of hair that clung to her face. "I remember being scared. It was nighttime. I want to say that there were others with me, but I can't see them.

Like there's a fog. It's like my brain is telling me I wasn't alone, but if that's the case, why can't I remember them?"

"You will in time," he assured her.

She sure hoped so. While she'd been content these last few weeks without knowing her past and getting over the migraines, she suddenly yearned to recapture the memories—good or bad —of her past so she knew who *she* was.

"I wanted to run," she continued. "I think I might have even tried. My memory is just so murky about the details. But I remember the terror. And the pain as I was slammed to the ground." She lifted her hands, turning them over to look at her palms. "I recall how the pavement cut into my hands. There was a broken bottle near. I reached for it to use as a weapon, but I couldn't grab it."

She fisted her hands and slid her gaze to Marshall. "I can't remember anything clearly after that. George tells me that I fended off the werewolf while it was trying to bite me."

"What color wolf?"

She blinked. "Color?"

"Yes. Every were is different. If you can recall the color, we might be able to find him or her."

"I don't know," she said, shaking her head.

He straightened and wrapped his arm around her again. "It doesn't matter. How long ago was this?"

"About eight weeks or so. George said I was out of it for a while."

"And they didn't get you to a doctor?"

She shrugged while wrinkling her nose. "Voodoo and all that. Delphine is apparently pretty powerful."

"And you trust her?"

"She saved me. Why wouldn't I trust her?"

He bowed his head. "Point taken."

"Do you not like her?"

"I've never met her."

"That's not what I asked," she pressed. "You don't necessarily have to meet someone to like them."

Marshall's smile was tight. "I've not heard very good things about her."

"And?" Riley pressed. "I hear an 'and' in there."

He stared at her a long moment. "She tried to hurt a few of my friends."

"I'm sorry. I didn't know. Delphine has only ever been good to me."

"Let's hope it remains that way."

Why then did Riley have a feeling that there was another meaning to his words? She wanted to press him for more, but there was a part of her that was a little scared of discovering anything else.

After all, she had thought Delphine bordered on sainthood. Now, she learned that the priestess had tried to hurt others. Riley wanted to say that perhaps Delphine was defending herself, but the words wouldn't come.

"You're thinking too hard," Marshall said.

The sound of the motor slowing made her sad. "The ride's over."

"That doesn't mean our day has to end."

She smiled and turned to face the city. But the sight of George and Delphine standing on the pier wiped the expression from her face.

"What is it?" Marshall asked. Then he followed her gaze. "Ah. I see."

Delphine had said she could do whatever she wanted for the day, so why were she and George there? It infuriated Riley. Especially since Delphine told her she wasn't a prisoner.

"Is he your boyfriend?" Marshall asked, referring to George.

Riley pulled Marshall behind a group of people. "He wants

to be. He won't take no for an answer," she replied, letting the frustration ring in her words.

"You don't have to go with them."

She stopped and faced him. "I do. I can't explain it, but I have to go. I need you to hide, though."

"Hide?" he asked with a quirk of his brow.

"Please."

He looked over her head to the shore before he gave a single nod. "I want to see you again."

"Tomorrow," she said. "There's a little store two streets over from the bench. Meet me there at two."

He pulled her against him for a quick kiss as the boat docked. Riley pulled away and shoved him back so he could hide.

In all the time she spent with Delphine, there had never been an occasion for her to lie to the priestess, so she wasn't sure why she did it now. Only that her gut told her to, and she trusted that instinct.

Riley looked back over her shoulder to have one more look at Marshall as she fell in line with the others to disembark, but he was now out of sight.

When she walked from the boat onto shore, she smiled when she saw Delphine and George. "What are you two doing here?"

"You left my area," Delphine said, disappointment tinting her words.

Riley widened her eyes. "I know. I wanted to push myself. I figured during the day would be better. I'm not that far from your section, so I knew I could get back if I needed to."

"And the man you were with?" George demanded as he looked at the face of every dark-haired man who exited the boat.

"I don't know who you're talking about.

Delphine raised a brow and folded her arms over her chest.

"George followed you today. He said you spoke with a man and took his hand."

Riley's first instinct was fury over being followed, but her gut told her not to show it. Not yet, at least. Instead, she gave a hollow laugh. "Oh, that man was a tourist. He was lost and looking for his way back to the French Quarter."

"That's not what it looked like," George said.

Delphine put an arm out, blocking him from advancing on Riley. The priestess's black eyes bored into her. "So, you weren't meeting anyone?"

"Who would I meet?" Riley said with a frown. "I'm alone except for you, my friends."

And her brothers.

The thought drew her up short. That was the second time in less than an hour that, for just an instant, she thought she had siblings, but she couldn't get any more from her memories than that. Not how many, not their names. Nothing.

"You had me worried," Delphine said with a sigh. "It's time to go home, child."

As Riley walked away with them, she had to fight not to look back for Marshall. Already she missed the safety of his arms —and the heat of his kiss.

7

*I*f Marshall thought not telling the Chiassons he had found their sister was hard, it was nearly impossible to keep from letting them know he had spent a few hours with her. Yet, somehow, he managed to keep his mouth shut.

Mainly because the things Riley had told him worried him greatly. She said she was able to do what she wanted, but there had been a healthy dose of fear in her eyes when she spotted Delphine and George.

Whatever the priestess was doing to Riley, it wasn't working fully. The truth seemed to be making itself known to her slowly and at odd moments, but it was coming back to Riley.

If he tried to tell her everything now, she might very well bolt and inform Delphine of it all, which would send the priestess after him. Frankly, Marshall would rather not go up against Delphine on his own.

He needed more time with Riley to slowly get the truth to reveal itself to her. Only then would she believe anything he had to say.

Thankfully, none of the Chiassons called him. It was a reprieve, but one he appreciated. Though he didn't get much sleep. He kept thinking about Riley's kisses and how he hadn't wanted to let her go. Ever.

He was literally counting down the minutes until he could see her again, to hold her. To taste her.

Night finally gave way to dawn, but his anxiety only grew. He couldn't shake off the sense that something had happened. A scan of the internet showed that while there had been crimes committed in New Orleans, none had involved anyone that fit Riley's description.

Why then did a feeling of dread fill him?

The morning crept by, during which he worked out and did more research on Delphine and the Voodoo culture. When noon finally came, he ate a quick meal before jumping into the shower. He was ready over an hour early, but he couldn't stay within the confines of the house anymore.

Marshall got into his truck and drove toward Delphine's area. He parked on the outskirts of the sector and decided to walk as he had the past two days. The violinist wasn't perform-ing, so he continued on until he found a pantomime.

With time to kill and an affinity for watching others, Marshall found a bench and sat. There was so much he could tell about someone just from a few minutes of observation. It was a skill he liked to hone. And it helped pass the time.

When it got closer to two, Marshall rose and found the store Riley had spoken of. He walked inside and picked up a handcart while leisurely strolling through the aisles. Since he needed a few things, he began to fill the basket. When he checked his watch, it was ten minutes after two. He glanced toward the door and discreetly walked down the center row to look down the aisles. But there was no sign of Riley.

He remained calm since she had been late the day before, as well. It was no great feat to position himself so that he could see the door and everyone who entered. He moved often so as not to draw attention to himself. Especially since any of those around him could be Delphine's followers.

The time stretched to three, and it became impossible to remain. He made his way to the cashier and got in line, thankful that there were people in front of him. Then, another cashier opened and motioned him to her. Marshall tapped the woman's shoulder in front of him and pointed out the waiting cashier. But not even that could stop him from eventually reaching his turn.

All too soon, he paid, and his groceries were bagged. Marshall was thankful that he hadn't bought anything that needed refrigeration because he didn't intend to leave yet. He walked around, keeping an eye out for Riley's tall form and dark locks.

Every time he caught a glimpse of someone who might be her, his heart raced. But disappointment soon reigned. The more time that passed with no sign of Riley, the more worried he became.

It was nearing five o'clock when he finally gave up and headed back to his truck. Anger and frustration and regret rolled through him in waves. Not to mention the heavy doses of fear that something had happened to Riley.

Two hours later, he'd nearly paced a hole in the floor of Donnie's house. Knowing he was probably going to regret it later, Marshall drove to Gator Bait. He only knew Kane and Solomon—barely—but if anyone knew the underbelly of the city, it was the four werewolves.

He parked on the side of the street and shoved a hand through his hair after he got out of the truck. The bar was situated in a prime corner location with the large wooden sign that looked as if a huge gator had taken a bite out of it.

Music from within wafted out onto the street. Loud, noisy

places weren't his particular cup of tea—unless it was for pool—but this was a necessity.

With a sigh, he walked across the street to the door and stepped over the threshold. A quick glance showed that every table was full with only a couple of barstools open. There were several pool matches going on, and all four dart boards were occupied. If he weren't there on business, he would have made his way over to a pool table and gotten involved in a match. But that was for another day.

"Find yourself a place," said a woman with long, black hair and dark, smoky eyes.

Based on Beau's description, that was Skye Parrish, Court LaRue's woman. It didn't take long for Marshall to locate Kane acting as bartender.

He walked to the bar and lowered himself onto the stool. When Kane's blue gaze landed on him, the werewolf froze. Marshall clasped his hands together on the glossy bar and gave a nod.

"What can I get you to drink?" Kane asked, studying him.

"Bourbon."

Kane raised a blond brow as he set a glass on the bar. "That kind of night, is it?"

"You've no idea."

After pouring the alcohol, Kane shoved the glass to him. "How about you share?"

"I'd love to."

Kane jerked his head to the side as he walked away. Marshall grabbed his glass and downed the whiskey before following. He wasn't surprised when Kane took him to the back of the bar and into the kitchen area before turning right to an office.

"Myles, you're going to want to get off the phone," Kane said as he motioned Marshall to a chair.

Marshall nodded to Myles and put his hands on the arms of

the chair before lowering himself down. When Myles hung up, Marshall said, "Hello."

"And you are?"

"Marshall Ducet."

"Ahh," Myles said, nodding. "The sheriff in Lyons Point. What the hell are you doing here?"

Kane said, "We all want to know that."

Solomon, the eldest LaRue, walked in, followed by the youngest, Court.

"Marshall," Solomon said. "I'm surprised to see you here. Can I hope this trip is one of pleasure?"

"Unfortunately not," Marshall said. He blew out a breath and pressed his lips together. "I wouldn't be here if it wasn't important, and I need all of you to understand that what I'm about to tell you, no one else can know."

Court crossed his arms over his chest. "We're waiting."

"It's about Riley, isn't it?" Kane asked, his blue eyes filled with worry.

Marshall cracked his knuckles and wished he had another shot of bourbon. "Yeah."

"Don't keep us in suspense," Myles said.

Unable to stay seated, Marshall rose to his feet. There wasn't much room to pace with the four brothers standing around the desk staring at him, but he couldn't keep still. He rubbed the back of his neck, giving himself one last second to make sure he was doing the right thing. Not that the LaRues would let him leave now that they knew what had brought him to New Orleans.

"Do my cousins know you're here?" Solomon asked.

Marshall glanced at him and walked a few steps before turning around. "They do. It was my suggestion not to alert any of you to my arrival."

"Why?" Court demanded.

Myles leaned back in his chair. "Because if we'd known, we would've pushed ourselves on his search, making it impossible for him to look on his own and thus drawing attention to him by being associated with us."

"You found her, didn't you?" Kane asked.

Marshall halted and looked at Kane. From what he'd heard, Riley and Kane became close friends after she arrived. They shared an apartment, which allowed Kane to keep an eye on her, and for her to keep an eye on him. The bond that developed between the two had stabilized Kane and given Riley purpose.

Marshall blew out a deep breath. "I did."

With two simple words, Solomon, Court, and Myles began bombarding him with questions.

"Is she all right?"

"Did you talk to her?"

"Why isn't she with you?"

"Do you have her hidden somewhere?"

"Can we see her?"

"When can we kick Delphine's ass?"

"Enough!" Kane bellowed, putting a stop to the questions.

Marshall looked at each of the brothers. "Riley is hale and hearty. But she's...not herself."

"How do you mean?" Myles asked as he braced his arms on his desk, a frown furrowing his brow.

Marshall struggled to find the words. "For one, she believes she doesn't have any family."

A look of fury erupted over Court's face. "What the fuck?"

Marshall held up his hand. "I came to the same conclusion that you four and the Chiassons did. Delphine had to have her. Since I don't register on the priestess's radar, I decided to stroll through the section of the city she's claimed as hers. Imagine my surprise when I saw Riley that first day."

"I think I'm going to be sick," Court mumbled.

Solomon's blond brows drew together in concern and disbelief. "The first day? You mean, you had only just begun looking for her, and she was there?"

"Yes," Marshall answered. "I walked over to the bench where she was sitting, and we had a nice chat. She told me that Delphine found her after an attack. That it's the priestess who's been sheltering her and keeping her safe."

"Actually, I know I'm going to be sick," Court stated.

Kane issued a growl to Court before turning his gaze back to Marshall. "What kind of attack?"

This was the part Marshall didn't want to tell them, but there was no way around it. "A werewolf attack."

The four brothers displayed varying degrees of shock. It was Solomon who clenched his fists at his sides and said, "It's so damn obvious. Of course, the bitch would make our cousin believe she was attacked by the very creatures we are so she won't trust us."

"We underestimated Delphine," Myles said with a shake of his head. "And how the hell did we do that after everything she's done to this family?"

Kane glanced at the ceiling. "So, the very thing we're trying to kill took Riley, somehow erased her memories of us and her brothers, made her believe she was attacked by a were, and now, Riley thinks Delphine is her friend."

"Yeah," Marshall said.

"It's probably a good thing you didn't tell Vin and the others. They would've been here immediately, wanting to attack Delphine," Solomon said.

Court issued a loud snort. "Hell, I want to attack her."

"You can't," Marshall said. "Not yet anyway."

"Then why did you come to us?" Myles inquired.

Marshall suddenly found that his legs couldn't hold him. He sank into the chair he'd abandoned moments ago. "Riley wanted me to meet her yesterday. She was followed by a black man named George. She didn't see him, but I was able to get us away. We even left Delphine's area and got on a tour boat. Her memory is there, but it's being blocked. I think she recalls things at times, but she questions them. Anyway, when we docked, Delphine and George were waiting for her."

"Did they see you?" Solomon asked.

He shook his head. "Riley asked me to hide, which I did. But we made plans to meet today. And that's what brought me here. She never showed up."

8

*H*er body was on fire. It burned from the inside out with desire that felt as if it would never be quenched. Yet Riley knew that there was one who could ease the ache within her—Marshall.

She tried to move, but her arms and legs were held down. Thrashing her head, she attempted to call out. But no sound fell from her lips.

Her hair tangled in her face. She felt it stick to her skin, just as she felt the wind whisper over her bare legs and the sweaty hands that pinned her down. The hard floor vibrated from the stomping and clapping of those around her, which was only matched by the loud singing.

Was this a nightmare? Because she couldn't remember any of her dreams being so... vivid. It had to be a nightmare. Otherwise, someone was doing this to her.

"Shh," a voice said near her ear. "Stop fighting."

Delphine. Riley recognized her voice and soft hands smoothing the hair away from her face. She stopped struggling, thinking that she might wake from this horrible dream.

Instead, she felt the hem of her gown being pushed up her

thighs to her hips, exposing her panties. Riley's heart began to pound as fear consumed her when she couldn't open her eyes.

"She's coming," Delphine whispered. "Open yourself up for the spirit to possess you, child."

No. Riley didn't want to be possessed. She, more than anyone, knew that doing such a thing opened a person up to all sorts of events afterward.

But wait. How was she so sure of that?

Lincoln had told her.

No sooner did she think of her brother than she felt someone over her. There was only a fraction of a second before the body rested atop hers.

Marshall. She could picture his face, recall the taste of his kiss, feel the heat of his body. He wouldn't let anyone hurt her. She was as sure of that as she was that—

"I want you."

George's rough, lust-filled voice made her panic, but now, she couldn't even move her head. She screamed as loud as she could in her brain as he ground his arousal against her, humping her.

"Now, Delphine?" he asked.

"Soon, my sweet. Soon, Riley will be yours. Until then, Elin awaits you."

Riley stopped chopping the bell pepper and lifted her gaze out the window.

"What's wrong?" Elin asked as she walked into the kitchen carrying a basket of homemade jams someone had delivered.

Riley looked over and met Elin's green gaze. "I just feel like I was supposed to do something today."

"You had a terrible migraine last night. I heard you call out."

How come she didn't remember that? "It must have been a bad one."

"You don't remember, do you?" Elin asked, her lips turning down in a frown.

Riley shook her head.

Elin walked to her and put a hand on her arm. "I was like that for months after Delphine found me. They'll go away, just like they did for me."

Months of pain and lost time? Riley wasn't sure she could stand another day of it, much less longer.

Something pulled at her mind again. She was sure she was supposed to be somewhere else. The more she fought to remember, the farther away the memory seemed to go.

"What's on your arm?" Elin asked.

Riley looked down and saw the bruise on her left wrist. A glance at her other arm showed the same thing. "I have no idea."

And that's what frightened her. Lost time, bruises she couldn't explain, and the feeling that she was forgetting something vitally important that plagued her.

"I did hear you yell," Elin said. "Maybe they had to restrain you."

Suddenly, a flash of images filled Riley's mind. They came at her so quickly that she dropped the knife and grabbed hold of the counter to remain standing.

Delphine leaning over her.

People holding her down.

George pulling up her gown.

George on top of her.

Then George having sex with Elin.

Riley jerked her head to her friend. Though she wouldn't be able to explain it, she knew those images weren't fragments of dreams. It had actually happened, but she couldn't say when or where.

Elin scrunched up her face as she took a step back. "Why are you looking at me like you know something that I don't?"

"Are you having sex with George?"

Elin's face went slack before her eyes widened. "What? No. He showed interest in me for a while, but then you came. Everyone knows he wants you."

"So you aren't sleeping with him?"

"No," Elin stated more firmly, her eyes hard. "I already said I wasn't. What's wrong with you today?"

Riley licked her lips. "I'm sorry. I don't know why I asked that."

The lie was an easy one since she used it often enough. But it was the first time it hadn't been the truth. Riley wanted to clutch her head and shake it. She began to wonder if her mind wasn't more affected by her attack than she originally thought. Perhaps she should talk to Delphine.

NO!

Her inner voice issued the bellow so loudly that Riley thought it had come from Elin for a second.

Riley backed away from the counter. She wished she could see the one person she did trust, M.... His name was on the tip of her tongue, but more troubling, was that she couldn't dredge up his image in her mind.

"I'm not feeling well," she told Elin. "I'm going to go lie down."

Elin nodded worriedly. "I'll be up shortly to look in on you."

Riley left the kitchen and started up the stairs. Halfway to her room, she looked down to find George at the bottom, staring at her with such a covetous expression that it sickened her.

Once in her room, Riley shut the door, only then noticing that there was no lock on it. She glanced around, but there was nothing that she could easily move to bar the entrance. Which meant that she would never sleep easy again.

What was going on that she was suddenly wary and nervous in a house where she had always felt safe?

Always?

Well, maybe not that long, but as long as she had been recovering.

She turned and walked to the bed. There, she lay down and threw an arm over her eyes. It took her several minutes before she was able to calm herself enough that her breathing evened out.

That's when she began going through every male name that she knew that started with the letter M. She got to the name Mark, and it gave her pause, but she knew it wasn't quite right. But it had to be similar.

So she started over, using all the "Mar" combinations she knew until she finally landed on it.

"Marshall," she whispered.

As soon as she said the name, she recalled their two meetings, the boat ride, the kiss, and her promise to meet him today at the market.

Riley jerked upright and looked at the clock on her nightstand to see that it was after five. She could try to get away, but George would only follow her. Hopefully, Marshall would return to the store tomorrow.

She had no way of contacting him, nor did she know where he lived. Everything rested on hoping that she could get away the next day and that he'd return.

Approaching footsteps had her quickly lying down again, though this time, she put her back to the door as she curled on her side. She waited when the footsteps paused outside her room for a few seconds before moving on.

Riley didn't so much as move a toe. She stared at the wall,

waiting to make sure no one was there, wondering all the while why she would forget Marshall. He was the one thing she wouldn't forget. He'd been charming, gorgeous, and nice. Not once had he hurt her or made her do anything she didn't want to do.

No matter how many migraines she had, none of them would make her forget a person. And then there were the flashes. They happened. She would bet her life on it. But she couldn't recall any more than those brief seconds she saw in her mind.

She looked down at her wrists and the bruises. Then she covered her left wrist with her right hand and found that the bruises lined up with her fingers. Which meant that someone had held her down.

Riley knew at that moment that she had to get away from Delphine, George, and the house. She didn't know who was involved and who to trust, and that meant she couldn't even tell Elin her thoughts.

Whatever was going on, she wanted to be far from it. Maybe then the migraines would stop, and she could remember things. Like... She fisted her hands. Something had happened yesterday on the boat with Marshall. She recalled a memory that had distressed her, but it was now gone from her recollection.

She sighed loudly.

Why wasn't she scared like Elin, who refused to go farther than Delphine's yard? No matter how much anyone coaxed her, Elin wouldn't go another step. She said it was her fear of another werewolf attack that kept her at Delphine's. Only now that Riley thought about it, Elin, like her, didn't have a bite from a were.

How was it that both were attacked yet neither of them sustained any type of injury?

Riley sat up and glanced at her door before looking out the window. It was too far of a drop for her to try and get out that way, and there was no way she could go out any of the doors without George knowing it.

He was always near, always watching. And, somehow, she knew that if she remained at the house, George would have her body—even if she didn't want him.

Once more, she had no proof of that, only a feeling, a sixth sense that she felt all the way to her soul. So she couldn't go to Delphine or Elin or anyone with her thoughts. No one would believe her.

But at least her memories of Marshall had returned. If she could get to him, then she had a chance. It was just finding him. And in a city the size of New Orleans, that might very well be impossible.

Riley didn't remain in her room long. To do so meant that Delphine would pay her a visit to check on her, so Riley rose and returned to the kitchen to finish preparing the evening meal. She ate with the others, keeping involved with the conversation while making sure never to look at George, who sat across from her. After she and Elin cleaned up, Riley went upstairs and took a long bath.

Thankfully, there was a lock on that door. She hated having to leave the bathroom, but others had need of it. Inside her room, she sat with her back against the wall, staring at the door. Waiting to see what would come for her.

9

*T*he Witching Hour was real. Marshall stood on the roof of Gator Bait with Kane as the other three LaRue brothers shifted and took up their posts throughout the city.

After spilling everything to the brothers, they had simply asked Marshall what he needed. The problem was, Marshall didn't have a clue. All he knew for sure was that he had to get to Riley.

And soon.

"Do you hear it?" Kane asked.

Marshall looked over at him. Kane stood as still as stone, his lips rarely lifting into a smile of any sort. All because of Delphine's curse, a curse that had made Kane her weapon against his will and changed him.

"Hear what?" Marshall asked as he strained to pick up whatever it was Kane heard.

Kane's blue gaze was directed toward Delphine's section. "Beneath the noise of the city beats the heart of magic. It's why New Orleans is a mecca for the supernatural. Anything magical lives and breathes here. Thrives. Magic drives everything. If you listen closely, you can hear it."

"I know it's there, but I don't feel it like you do."

"You may be lucky in that regard."

Marshall wondered what Riley was doing. Years on the job and encountering all sorts of vile people allowed him to imagine dozens of ways Delphine could be hurting her. "I don't consider myself lucky to not be able to fight the supernatural."

"You're fighting." Kane swiveled his head to him, pinning him with his ice blue eyes that flashed yellow, showing the wolf within. "You fought while you were a detective here, and you fight alongside my cousins."

"It's not like I do much good. I've learned a few things from the Chiassons, but I'm not nearly as skilled."

Kane let out a long breath as he resumed his watch. "In many ways, I envy my cousins. If anything supernatural arrives in Lyons Point, they immediately hunt it. We don't have that option here since this is a Safe City."

Safe City meaning that any supernatural creature could find solace there—as long as they obeyed the rules. If they didn't, then the LaRues would hunt them down and kill them.

"Your job is very much like mine," Marshall said. "I can usually pick out the ones who are going to be trouble, but I have to wait for them to do something before I can arrest them."

Kane shook his head slowly. "Then you have the ultimate monsters like Delphine. The one time she was weak enough that we could've taken her out was when we were just boys, and she killed our parents. If she hadn't run off the Moonstone pack, we could've ended this."

"She's smart. I'll give her that," Marshall admitted.

"In all my life, she's the one thing I've feared." Kane drew in a deep breath. "The only other person who knows that is Riley."

Marshal glanced at Kane. "I don't think less of you for being afraid of Delphine. She cursed you."

"And has wreaked havoc on everyone in my family. It has to stop."

"It will."

Kane rotated his shoulders as if it was killing him to stand still. But the brothers alternated, and it was his turn to stay behind. "Will it? Or will Delphine finally triumph? She has the one thing neither our cousins nor we will harm. And because of that, she has the ultimate control."

"Not if I can talk to Riley again."

The were's gaze returned to him. "You sound confident. Why?"

"Riley and I had a connection."

"Apparently a serious one by the way you gave a slight pause before saying it."

Damn. Kane would've been a great detective. Marshall decided there was no need to go into detail. "Yes."

Kane raised a brow, his gaze knowing. "I see."

"Riley is special."

"Very much so. A lot of people are putting their faith in you. Don't get in Delphine's crosshairs, and don't get killed."

"It isn't my plan."

Kane's face went cold. "It wasn't mine to be cursed either."

"One way or another, Riley and I will meet again."

"It's time we don't have. The longer Delphine has her hooks in Riley, the harder it will be to bring my cousin back."

Marshall put his hand on his hip where the holster of his gun usually hung. He had a pistol in his truck, and he wished he were wearing it.

"There might be something you can do to help," Kane said.

He turned to the werewolf. "Name it."

"When we hunted together, I taught Riley the symbol my brothers and I learned from my parents. We mark it on things to let each other know where we've been. The sigil is altered slightly for each of us, and I made Riley her own."

Marshall nodded, liking what he was hearing. "That sounds good, but how is it going to help?"

"Put it someplace Riley goes often. Then leave a trail that will bring her to you. If she recognizes the symbols, she'll find her way."

"That could work."

Kane squatted and looked down at the street below where a man was following three girls. "You'll be on your own. We'll head into Delphine's district to keep their attention on us, but we won't be able to mark anything."

"Understood."

"Good," Kane said right before he jumped from the third-story roof to the ground behind a man.

Even from the distance, Marshall heard Kane's growl as he landed. The man whirled around and attacked. That's when Marshall saw the guy's red eyes, signaling him as a vampire. In seconds, Kane ended his life as the three women walked on without ever knowing they were in danger.

Riley fought to keep her eyes open. It felt so good to close them, but her life depended on remaining awake. She glanced over at the bedside table to the clock that read 1:57.

This night was the longest of her life. She yawned and stood to get the blood flowing. That's when she saw something outside through her window. She immediately recognized Delphine's form in her usual all white, and George, walking shirtless beside her toward the vacant house. They were talking when George looked up at Elin's window.

Delphine was the first inside the darkened dwelling. Within

minutes, candles along the windowsills were lit, casting everything in a soft glow.

Riley's head jerked to the side. Elin was in the room next to hers, and she was now moving around. Riley silently tiptoed to the wall that separated them and put her ear against it, listening.

The sound of Elin's door opening had Riley yanking her ear away as she looked at her own door. The floorboards creaked as Elin made her way past Riley's room to the stairs.

Riley's heart pounded as she debated whether or not to follow. Elin could be going to get something to drink. Or it could be something much, much worse.

The image of Elin and George having sex flashed in Riley's mind again.

She squeezed her eyes shut and shook her head to dislodge the scene, but it held fast. Then she moved to the side of her window and looked out, praying that Elin remained in the house.

But it wasn't long before she spotted the woman making her way toward Delphine and George.

Riley didn't hesitate this time. She quietly left her room and hurried down the stairs. When she reached the back door, she opened it just wide enough to slip through before softly closing it behind her.

She flattened herself against the house, looking across the yard to the abandoned structure. For some reason, Riley's hatred of the dwelling grew. She didn't want to go near it, but she had to. For Elin.

Looking all around her to make sure no one was about, Riley darted across the lawn to the other residence and once again flattened herself against the support.

She didn't know how she knew to do these things, only that they came naturally to her. As if she had learned them years ago.

Whatever the reason, they were aiding her now, so she was thankful.

Listening carefully, she could hear Delphine talking to Elin, but couldn't quite make out what was said. With the house on piers, she couldn't easily look through the windows since she couldn't reach them. But that didn't stop her.

Riley began searching for something to climb up on to allow her to see inside. After a bit of searching, she found a cinderblock and carried it back to the window. Then she stood on it and peeked inside.

She was so shocked to find Elin standing naked in the middle of the room surrounded by dozens of candles on the floor that Riley jerked back, falling off her makeshift step. It would be so easy to return to the safety of her room, but Elin was her friend. How could she leave now?

With her mind set, Riley climbed back on the block and resumed her watch.

Delphine stood at the front of the room with her eyes closed as she sang. George then walked to stand beside Elin. He grabbed a fistful of Elin's long, dark hair and yanked hard. Elin kept her gaze on him, never flinching or crying out.

"Get on your knees," George ordered.

Elin dropped down, waiting. Riley couldn't look away as George demanded she remove his pants and then take him into her mouth. By the vacant look in Elin's eyes, she had no idea what she was doing.

Riley closed her eyes and gagged, even as she wondered if they had done the same thing to her. She forced herself to look back at Elin.

George now had her on her back, her legs spread. The glee on his face at his total domination of Elin sickened Riley. She knew then that her *dream* of George grinding against her had been real.

And it put into question everything Riley believed. More than anything, she no longer trusted Delphine. How could she when the priestess was part of such horrors?

Riley covered her mouth as George claimed Elin, taking her body roughly. Tears spilled down her cheeks. It was all Riley could do not to bust inside the house and kill George and Delphine—but something held her back.

A deep-rooted fear that loudly cautioned her to be careful.

Riley stepped off the cinderblock and returned it to where she'd found it, and then she stealthily made her way back to her room. There, she stood watch next to her window, hidden from view as she waited for them to finish with Elin.

It was after 4:30 before George and Delphine escorted Elin up to her room. As soon as Riley saw them exit the other residence, she slid beneath her covers and curled on her side, anxiously waiting as she focused all her energy on her hearing. Every sound in the house was as loud as a rocket, but none more so than the footsteps leading up the stairs and past her door.

Minutes after they'd *tucked* Elin into bed, Riley heard her door open. She kept her breathing even, and her eyes closed even though she was screaming inside.

Her blood ran cold when two sets of footsteps approached her. Soft fingers ran along her cheek. She wanted to jerk away, to plunge a knife into their hearts, anything but lie there and let them do as they wished.

"I ache for her," George said.

Delphine slid her long fingers into Riley's hair. "It's not quite time. She's fighting this harder than Elin. We can't push her too soon, or we could break her. And I've need of her yet."

"I have need of her."

"Your lust is never-ending."

George's voice lowered in anger. "Don't fuck with me, priestess. You gave me this body to possess, but you don't rule me. I'm tired of waiting for Riley. I want her. Make it happen tomorrow night. Or you won't like the consequences."

"But the La—"

"I don't care about the werewolves. You'll find another way to wipe them out. I've chosen Riley as mine."

With that, George strode from the room. It was several more tense minutes before Delphine followed.

Even after her door was shut, Riley didn't move. While she had been fighting sleep earlier, she couldn't sleep now if her life depended on it. She counted down five minutes and didn't hear anything. Finally, she opened her eyes a slit and looked around before she sat up and leaned against the iron headboard.

Without a doubt, she and Elin had to get away.

Tomorrow.

10

The LaRues commanded attention. Marshall was never more aware of the brothers' reach than observing everyone in Delphine's district watching them as they paired off and walked the streets.

Those staring after the LaRues were Delphine's followers—and there were many.

Marshall tossed money into the case of the violinist who had returned and made his way to the market where he was supposed to meet Riley the day before. He'd already left the symbol Kane taught him on the bench with an arrow pointed toward the store. Outside the building, he hastily drew a circle within a circle, making sure the lines met on the left side. Then he added another arrow.

It took Marshall forty-five minutes before he was finished in Delphine's district, marking the symbols discreetly. A text to Kane let him know the LaRues could leave, but they were using the opportunity to search for their cousin.

Two hours later, Marshall carved the last of the symbols on the lamppost on the sidewalk outside of Donnie's house. Marshall looked back, hoping that Kane's suggestion worked.

Otherwise, Marshall might go knocking on every door searching for Riley. Because he wasn't sure how long he could wait before he saw her again.

Her theatre teacher would've been proud, especially since Riley had all but failed the class in high school. Yet, she'd become a master that morning when she left her room and proceeded as she had every other day that she could remember.

She looked for minute details in everyone to catch anything that would tell her they didn't buy her act. But so far, so good.

Unfortunately, she didn't get time alone with Elin until after lunch. They sat out in the back yard beneath the cloudy sky sipping ice tea.

"Why do you keep looking at me like that?" Elin asked.

Riley rubbed her finger along the condensation of her glass before taking a long drink of the sweet tea. "How did you sleep last night?"

"Like a baby."

"Did you get up?"

Elin rolled her eyes. "No. What's going on?"

"I have to tell you something, and I'm afraid you won't believe me."

Elin turned her head to look at Riley. "We'll never know the answer to that unless you tell me."

Riley knew she was right, yet once the words were out, there was no putting them back. And there was a chance that Elin would tell Delphine.

But Riley would be long gone by then.

"Yesterday, when I asked if you were having sex with George, it was because I saw you."

Elin's brows grew together, half in shock, half in denial. "I think I'd know if I was giving my body to someone."

"I also remembered being held down as he ground into me." Riley held up her hands to show the bruise again. "Then there was the fact that I was supposed to meet someone yesterday, but I forgot all about them."

Elin turned her whole body to face Riley. "Who were you meeting?"

"Did you hear the part where I said I couldn't remember them?"

"Yes," Elin nodded slowly, anxiety growing in her eyes.

Riley licked her lips and pushed onward. "Something within me told me there was something wrong. I stayed awake all night because I had a feeling something would happen. And it did. But not to me."

It took a moment, but Elin's eyes widened as realization dawned. "Me? It happened to me?"

"Yes."

Elin looked forward again and swallowed. "Do you recall things that don't make sense? Like having a family even though I know there's no one looking for me?"

"Brothers," Riley admitted. "I think I have brothers, but I don't know their names or faces or even how many."

Elin looked at her with widening eyes, nodding. "I have brothers. Two of them."

"You remember?"

"Just now, after you said something."

Riley smiled and reached across to grab Elin's hand. "That's good."

"Tell me about last night."

With those words, Riley's grin faded, and she released Elin. "I saw George and Delphine head there," she said, nodding toward the adjacent house. "Candles were lit, and then you walked out of your room."

"No," Elin said as she scooted to the end of the chair.

Riley continued. "You walked from the house to where Delphine and George were. And I followed. I could hear Delphine singing, but I had to see. So I looked through the window."

"And?" Elin demanded when Riley paused.

Riley glanced away. "You were naked. George came to stand before you and ordered you first on your knees to remove his pants and then to take him into your mouth."

Elin slowly fell back on the chair. "And then he took me."

"You were aware?"

"No. Those images come to me through a thick fog, like a dream. They've been going on for months, but I didn't think they were real."

Riley leaned close and said. "I don't know what they're doing to us or why, but I think we need to leave. Now. Today."

"Yes. I want to find my brothers. And to stop the dreams."

Riley was about to tell Elin her plan when Delphine exited the house. She wore a bright smile as her long, black braids fell past her hips.

"Are you two enjoying the day?" Delphine asked.

Riley forced a smiled. "As much as we can before the rain comes."

Delphine kept her gaze on Elin. "And how about you, Elin? How are you feeling?"

"Fine," Elin replied, but she couldn't quite meet Delphine's gaze.

Riley watched as Delphine's brow furrowed. She then leaned over Elin and put her hand on her stomach. Riley's heart fell to her feet.

"What is it?" Elin asked as she moved the priestess's hand away.

Delphine straightened, a huge smile on her face. "Life is growing inside you, child."

"That's not possible," Elin said, her face going white.

"With Voodoo, anything is possible," Delphine said and turned on her heel. "I'll spread the news."

Elin turned to Riley once Delphine was out of earshot and said, "I can't stay here another second."

Riley tried to reach for her, but Elin was already up and running into the house. She hurriedly followed in time to see Elin collide with George in the kitchen. Riley prayed Elin would keep going, but the anger and betrayal were too much to contain. Elin confronted George. She barely got two words out before he had her by her throat up against the wall.

Elin looked at Riley. Riley glanced at the set of knives, contemplating using one as a weapon when she noticed one was missing.

"Run!" Elin shouted to Riley as she plunged the blade into George's chest.

Riley took a step toward her friend, but the crack of Elin's neck halted her. Riley watched as Elin fell to the ground in slow motion. Then Riley looked back at George, who pulled the knife from his chest without so much as flinching.

Shouts and approaching footsteps filled Riley's ears as loudly as a rushing wave. She gave Elin one last look before she turned and ran out the door. Knowing how everyone was a follower of Delphine kept Riley off the streets, moving between houses and ducking behind anything that could keep her hidden.

So many times she was sure someone had seen her, but miraculously, she was able to keep moving without being stopped—or chased. For once, she was happy when the rain began. She stole an umbrella from a porch and opened it, mingling with the others on the sidewalk. She kept her head down and walked as quickly as she could without bringing notice to herself.

Riley had no idea where she was headed. Though she wasn't surprised to find herself near the bench where she had first met Marshall. She paused to look at it. The rain sent everyone for cover, including the violinist. With a sigh, Riley continued on, not stopping again until she was in front of the market.

She glanced inside, hoping she might spot Marshall within, but he wasn't to be found. Just as she was turning away, something caught her eye. The symbol was no bigger than the palm of her hand, and though she couldn't say how she recognized it, she did. And she was sure it hadn't been there before.

The arrow pointed in the direction she was headed, so she decided to follow it. All the while, she kept her eye out for more of the symbols. And as luck would have it, she found them, each pointing her a certain direction.

The heavier the rain came, the more people hurried indoors. It allowed her to find the symbols easily enough. She shivered as her jeans from the thighs down were damp, and her bright pink Converse were soaked through.

As soon as she walked out of Delphine's section, she breathed a sigh of relief. That's when she began moving more quickly from symbol to symbol. Yet, she wasn't stupid. She stopped often, taking cover and looking behind her to see if she were being followed. Because she knew Delphine would come for her.

She ached for Elin's needless death, and she was terrified of what awaited her if Delphine—or George—found her. It's what kept her moving instead of hunkering down in a corner somewhere and letting the tears fall.

Because Riley wanted to make sure she wasn't followed, it

took her hours before she found herself standing in front of a house. This was where the symbols had led her.

Suddenly, the door opened, and a man stepped onto the porch. Her gaze collided with gray orbs. When she saw it was Marshall, her composure crumbled. Without a word, he walked into the rain and down the path to her before pulling her into his arms.

"I've got you," he said.

She clung to him, soaking in his warmth and his strength. He took the umbrella and turned them. With his arm around her, he walked her to the porch and then inside the house.

He led her to the bathroom and turned on the shower. "I'll leave some dry clothes on the bed for you. Take your time."

Riley only stayed beneath the hot water until she was warm. She dried off and found the sweat pants and tee shirt waiting for her. Then she went looking for Marshall. She found him in the living room, staring out the window.

He smiled when he saw her. "I wasn't sure you'd find your way here."

"I don't know what to believe anymore. I've seen...some horrible things, and I know Delphine has been lying to me."

The smile faded as a frown took its place. "What do you mean?"

She lifted her arms to show him the bruises.

"Who did that?" He was careful to keep his face even, but his words were laced with fury.

"I'm not sure. I only recall bits and pieces, but I know I was held down."

"Did they...hurt you?"

"I don't think so. But they did harm Elin."

He ran a hand down his face. "There was another woman with you?"

"She's dead because I told her I saw them taking her last night. Then Delphine told Elin she was pregnant."

Marshall closed the distance between them and put his hands on her arms. "Is that why you didn't meet me yesterday?"

"I didn't meet you because they made me forget you."

"But you remembered," he said, his face softening.

Riley grinned. "I couldn't forget you for long. But I want to know who I am."

"I can tell you that."

She released a thankful breath. "I was hoping you'd say that."

11

*M*arshall would never know what made him walk to the front of the house and look out the window. But when he'd seen Riley, he felt a rush of relief so great that it made his knees buckle.

He'd managed to catch hold of the back of a chair before he hit the ground, but that was only because he had wanted to get to Riley quickly. It took all of his control to calmly open the door instead of rushing out to her. The look of fear on her face made him want to hurt the ones responsible—and he intended to do just that.

Marshall hadn't cared about the rain when he walked out to her. He was immensely grateful when she didn't push his arms away, and instead, let him hold her before leading her into the house.

He walked around the house trying to find something to do while Riley warmed up beneath the hot water, but all his mind could focus on was wondering how she had gotten away from Delphine.

And when the priestess would come for her.

Marshall needed to call Kane and the others, but he wanted to talk to Riley more before he bombarded her with family that she didn't remember.

Then—*finally*—Riley was standing before him once more. She was no longer shivering, but as soon as she showed him her bruises, he found it nearly impossible not to go out into the storm and start bellowing for Delphine.

Riley wanted to know who she was. And it was up to him to tell her.

They sat in the living room facing each other in opposite chairs. He was sure someone else would be better at filling her in on her past, but he was selfish and didn't want anyone else with them.

"Is something wrong?" she asked.

He gave a shake of his head. "No."

"You're just sitting there. Normally, that means there's something you don't want me to know. At least that's been my experience with others."

Marshall ran a hand through his damp hair. "That's because I'm probably not the one who should be telling you about yourself."

"Why?" she asked with a frown, cocking her head to the side. "I thought you knew me."

Shit. He'd really stepped in it this time. "I know your brothers."

"So I do have brothers," she said with a grin. "I knew it! How many?"

"Four."

"Four!" she repeated with wide eyes. She looked at the ceiling and laughed. "Four."

He watched her curiously. "You're the youngest, which makes them very protective of you."

Her blue eyes returned to him. "Beau. That's one of my brothers' names."

"Yes," he replied, unable to stop the smile that pulled at his lips.

"Tell me more," she urged eagerly. "Why aren't they here?"

Each time Marshall tried to answer her question, he realized she needed to know more before she could fully comprehend what he was saying.

Finally, he said, "They looked for you extensively, but Delphine wants to hurt them. That's why I came instead. She doesn't know me."

"And she knows my brothers," she replied with a nod.

"Yes."

"How long have I been gone?"

He swallowed. "Over eight weeks."

"I see," she murmured and sighed.

"There was an attack, but not like you were led to believe. You were fighting with others against Delphine."

Riley's face shuttered as if she were searching her memories. "I don't recall that. Tell me more. How was I fighting her? Who were the others?"

Marshall rose and began to pace. He'd delivered all kinds of news to people before, but this time, he couldn't find the words. Because it was Riley.

Because he cared about her.

"Marshall," she said, standing before him so he had to halt. "I can handle whatever it is you don't want to tell me."

"It's not that I don't want to tell you, it's that there are years of information that bitch took from you. Things you lived through and did. My words won't be the same."

She put a hand on his arm and smiled. "But they may lead me to those memories."

He knew she was right, but he also knew that it should be

one of her brothers talking to her right now and not him. Yet, he was prepared to fight anyone—even Delphine—to remain by Riley's side.

"Your family fights the supernatural. Any evil that comes into the parish, your family hunts down and kills."

She blinked, nodded. "Wow. Tell me more."

"You were raised by your brothers when your parents were killed. Vin sent you off to Austin to attend college, and after you got your degree, you came to New Orleans."

Her gaze narrowed. "Why New Orleans? What's here? I wouldn't just randomly pick a place."

"Your cousins are here."

She looked away, her brow furrowed. "I...think my cousins are men, but I feel like there are women I'm close to, as well."

"You're very close to the women who have fallen in love with your cousins."

Her smile was back in place when she looked at him. "More memories are being unveiled, but it's going slow and only frag-ments at a time."

"Delphine had a lot of time to work her magic on you and wipe away all that you knew."

"She might have won had I not met you."

He tucked her wet hair behind her ear. "You're much too strong for Delphine to have kept a hold on you much longer."

"You know me, which means we did meet before."

"I wish we had, but I only saw you once. I'm the sheriff in Lyons Point, and I help your brothers when I can. I came to the house when you were leaving to return to New Orleans. We briefly looked at each other, but we never spoke."

She raised her brows. "How stupid of me."

"I know you, Riley, because I've listened to stories from your brothers. They sent me so many pictures of you from throughout your life that I almost feel as if I were with you all those years."

She glanced at his mouth, making his balls tighten. "How lucky my family is to have you as a friend, but I think I'm the really lucky one."

His blood rushed in his ears. He put a hand on her hip and lowered his head. "From the moment I saw you, I wanted to pull you close. Nothing would stop me from finding you. Not this city, not Delphine, and not magic."

"Here I am. In your arms," she murmured as she lifted her face to his.

Their lips brushed. He kissed her softly even as his body demanded he bury himself inside her. But as she moaned and sank against him, an image of her bruises popped into his mind. Marshall put his hands on her shoulders and ended the kiss.

She blinked up at him, confusion filling her gorgeous eyes. "What?"

"It wouldn't be right for me to do this without knowing if someone...if...."

"Raped me?" she finished.

He gave a nod.

She cupped his face. "I want you. The past doesn't matter. The future doesn't matter. This moment does. And I ache for you."

He was powerless when she pulled his head down to continue their kiss. And as soon as their tongues touched, he was lost in a sea of desire, swept beneath the tidal wave to surrender to the siren that had captured him, body and soul.

Fire burned through him, heating his skin until he was consumed. And it was all because of Riley. Her kisses were as sweet as honey and as scorching as a desert. Yet he couldn't get enough.

His hands moved around to her back, holding her close as he

plundered her mouth, his kiss fiery. She pressed against him, trying to mesh their bodies closer.

Marshall knew exactly how she felt. So when she tugged at his shirt, he reached to yank it off.

And then someone pounded on the door.

They jerked apart, breathing heavily as they stared at the front of the house. He glanced to where the rifle was behind Riley. Pointing to it, he put his finger to his lips and motioned for her to grab it. Once it was in her hands, he palmed the pistol he had hidden near the door and put it behind his back. Then he opened the portal a crack. His gaze met bright blue ones.

Kane lifted a dark blond brow. "You going to let me in?"

"What are you doing here?" Marshall asked, looking over Kane's shoulder.

"I thought you might want some company. Actually, that's a lie. I'm here because you were the last one to see Riley, so that means you're the best hope of finding her."

Marshall glanced over his shoulder to Riley behind him, who held the rifle pointed at the door like someone who knew how to use it. He then stepped back and widened the gap.

Kane took a step inside and came to an immediate stop. As soon as his gaze landed on Riley, he stared for a moment before glaring at Marshall.

"What the fuck?" Kane growled.

Riley lifted the rifle to her shoulder. "Marshall?"

"Easy," he told her. "Lower the gun. And look at him."

It took her a moment, but Riley did as he asked. She propped the weapon against the wall and stared hard at Kane for a long time.

"Riley," Kane said as he took another step toward her. "You know me. Search your mind."

She gave a shake of her head. "There's nothing there, no memory of you."

Marshall closed the door. "Don't try so hard." Then to Kane, he said, "Try sharing a memory with her."

"Right," Kane said as he glanced Marshall's way.

Riley watched him skeptically, as if she wasn't sure she wanted Kane in the house with them. But she remained, waiting.

"Around Christmastime, when the weather dropped into the thirties, you wanted ice cream at midnight. We went out in—"

"The rain," Riley interrupted him. "You found a place that was open, and we ate ice cream together."

Kane nodded, his face tight.

A tear rolled down Riley's face. "Kane," she said and rushed to him.

Marshall watched the stoic LaRue envelop his cousin in his arms and squeeze his eyes closed as he held her. The two remained that way for several minutes.

Then Riley pulled back and turned her gaze to Marshall. "I remember."

"All of it?" Kane asked worriedly.

She gave a nod. "All of it. Including what Delphine did to me."

"What did she do?" Kane's voice had lowered, his eyes flashing yellow.

Marshall kept his gaze on Riley. "And?"

"No," she whispered, smiling.

He let out a sigh, glad that Riley understood what he was asking.

Kane looked between them. "What the hell are you two talking about?"

"He wanted to know if I had been raped."

Marshall winced at Riley's words. She didn't realize how protective her cousins were of her. By the growl rumbling in Kane's chest, though, she got a reminder.

"I'm fine," Riley told him.

Marshall fisted his hands to stop from reaching for her each time her gaze landed on him. Would it be rude if he kicked Kane out of the house so he could have Riley to himself, and they could resume their kissing?

*D*elphine stared down at Elin's lifeless body. Everything she had worked years to achieve had been wiped away in seconds. Because of George.

His obsession with Riley had clouded his mind, making him forget the goals they had set together.

"Elin was carrying your child," she said.

"Riley is who I wanted to have my seed."

Delphine glared at him. "And now she's gone after witnessing this."

"I'll get her back," he stated.

"Perhaps it's better if you remain behind. She'll be frightened of you. It is why she ran."

George's lips turned into a sneer. "You have twenty-four hours, priestess, or I go looking for her myself."

Delphine turned and walked from the house. The streets were lined with her followers, each awaiting orders. They ignored the rain, standing without umbrellas or coats. This was New Orleans, and the rain came as often as the heat.

She removed her headscarf and let her hair down. Then she

made her way from the porch down the steps and out into her people, walking among them.

"You all know Riley Chiasson. I took her from the LaRues when they attempted to best me. She is mine now. I've taken her memories so that she believes she's without family. We're her family. But she's scared.

"We must find her and bring her home. She has yet to fulfill her role, and until she's back among us, she never will. Spread out, search for her all through the city. Go to the LaRues—their homes and their bar—and watch them. I want to know of any increased activity that means they might know where Riley is."

She stopped and turned in a circle to look at the faces that came to her for advice and help. These were the ones who would aid her in wiping the LaRues and Chiassons from this world for good.

"We need to find her before the LaRues do. Go!" she commanded.

As one, they all turned and spread out, doing her bidding.

Delphine watched them until they disappeared, then she turned back to her house. George stood on the porch, watching her. He had been her greatest achievement. One of her most faithful followers, he had opened himself up to the spirit of a famed Voodoo priest who had been cut down by the LaRues before he could carry out his grand plan.

With him by her side, Delphine knew she was unstoppable. He added to her already impressive depth of magic, and they had worked together perfectly. Until Riley.

As soon as he had seen her, desire had ruled George. He wouldn't listen to Delphine as she tried to explain that Riley was stronger than Elin, and it had taken Elin months to fully succumb to Delphine's magic.

Riley would take even longer, and to push her too soon

would break her. Or return her memories. And neither option was one Delphine wanted.

George turned on his heel and walked back into the house. Delphine sighed and blinked the rain from her eyelashes. If only he had been patient, he could've had a child from both Elin and Riley.

Delphine looked over her shoulder toward the French Quarter. The LaRues continued to find ways to best her. They had come so close this last time. Minka was incredibly strong, much stronger than Delphine had ever dreamed she could be.

That had nearly cost her everything. But Delphine wouldn't underestimate Minka or the LaRues again. Because they too were growing stronger.

At least she had stopped the Moonstone clan in their tracks. Taking Elin had brought her Griffin. The Alpha had done everything she wanted in exchange for keeping Elin alive. Griffin had been stronger than both his parents put together, but he'd let family and love rule him. Now, he was gone, having slunk away with his tail between his legs, no doubt.

One werewolf down. And with Griffin gone, the Moonstone pack was floundering. Now, all Delphine needed to do was take care of the LaRues and Chiassons.

She rubbed her hands together, calling up ancient magic from her African ancestors. She began humming, allowing herself to grow louder and louder.

"Find me Riley," she whispered.

She turned in a circle, waiting for the magic to direct her. But nothing happened. She attempted the ritual twice more no better results. Yet she wouldn't give up. There were many more tricks up Delphine's sleeve. She would find Riley, and if she had to slaughter each and every person in New Orleans, she would bring the girl back into the fold.

Marshall carefully lifted Riley in his arms and stood. She had fallen asleep between him and Kane thirty minutes earlier. Once Kane left to do a sweep of the area, Marshall knew it was time to get her in bed.

Her eyes opened when he laid her down. "Stay with me."

As if he could resist such a request—or the temptation. He climbed in beside her and smiled when she snuggled against him. It felt so good to hold her.

"I wish I would've talked to you that day I first saw you," she said.

"Why didn't you?"

"I knew you were the type of man I'd fall hard for. And the kind who could break my heart."

He looked down at the top of her head. "Why do you think I'd hurt you?"

"You're very much like my brothers and cousins. You're used to taking charge and risking your life. You think of others before yourself. It's a great quality, but it can be hell on relationships."

"Your brothers seem to make it work."

She nodded. "Yes, they do."

"So do your cousins. Well, except for Kane."

Her head lifted, and she shot him a grin. "I have hope for Kane. He has a big heart, but it's filled with so much hurt and regret right now. The right woman could change him."

"The right woman could do a lot of things," Marshall said as he held her gaze.

She glanced down as she came up on her elbow. "The way I feel when you kiss me is like I'm flying through the clouds."

"It's like coming home."

"Your kiss sears me to my very soul."

He ran his hand up her back to tangle his fingers in her hair. "You slay me. I want nothing but you. Only you."

"Always you," she murmured.

He cupped the back of her head as their lips met. As their tongues dueled, he rolled her onto her back and settled between her legs. She moaned in contentment.

Marshall rose up on his knees and removed the shirt. When she rose from the bed and began to strip, he quickly did the same.

As soon as their clothes were gone, they were back in each other's arms, kissing. He smiled when she pushed him backward onto the bed. Her blue eyes were dark with desire. With her dark hair falling haphazardly about her, he took in her slender form, and the pert breasts with their dusky nipples that he yearned to taste.

His gaze traveled down to her smooth belly and slim hips to the trimmed patch of black curls between her long legs.

"Keep looking," she said huskily while rubbing her hands over his chest. "I get to look at your amazing body."

Marshall felt as if he had waited his entire life to have her. He wrapped an arm around her and yanked her close. Searching her eyes, he looked for...hell, he didn't know what it was he wanted to find.

"It was your kiss," she told me. "You began to unravel all that Delphine had done. And you took me down a road I'd never been on before. Take me again."

"Yes," he whispered before he kissed her slowly, thoroughly.

He ran his hands up her back, learning the feel of her warm skin. Her hips rocked against him. God, she felt so good. Like she had been made just for him. Or maybe it was the other way around. Maybe he'd been made for her. Marshall didn't care.

As long as he got to have her.

"If I don't have you inside me right this instant, I might die," she said between kisses.

All thoughts he had of going slow and kissing every inch of her went right out the window. The need in her words, and the way her voice turned raspy from desire sent him careening into a haze of hunger only she could quench.

She had never *ached* so in her life. It went bone deep. Riley didn't fight it, she accepted it, reached for it. Grabbed it.

Whatever *it* was, it was amazing. Surprising.

Mind-blowing.

With every kiss, every touch and sigh, she could actually feel herself growing closer to Marshall. It defied logic, but she came from a world with the supernatural. Who was she to question such things? Which was why she marveled at her fortune and ate up every millisecond.

Because it could all end in the next minute.

But she wasn't going to think about Delphine or the epic battle she knew was coming. Instead, she would glory in the magnificent man beneath her.

She ran her hands over the thick sinew of his chest and the dark hair that covered him. The quick glance she'd gotten of his chiseled abs and corded arms and legs was forgotten when she saw his thick arousal.

There would come a time—really soon—when she paid that particular member a lot of attention.

Her breathing quickened, and her mind went blank when his hands moved over her ass and held her as he ground himself against her.

She gasped, her sex clenching as desire spun wildly through

her. Her inhale turned into a moan when his fingers found her. He slipped two inside, pumping slowly.

"There are so many things I want to do to you," he said in her ear before he nipped at her lobe.

She shivered from his words, his bite, and the way his fingers played her. Riley wanted to reply, to tell him that she wanted him to do all of them and more, but the words were lost as he pushed his fingers deeper.

"Is this what you want?"

She nodded, her throat refusing to form the words.

"Or is it this?"

His fingers left her. In the next instant, she felt the head of his cock rubbing against her swollen clit before he slipped inside her. As their bodies merged, it was like a key fitting into a lock.

She braced her hands on his chest and sat up. Their gazes clashed, held. With his hands on her hips, she began to slowly rock back and forth.

There was nothing that could stop their passion now. It hadn't just taken them. It consumed them. And through it all, though every tingle of pleasure, each quiver of need—she rushed toward it eagerly.

As her tempo increased, Marshall sat up. His silvery gaze raked her face as if he couldn't believe she was there. She understood how he felt because she feared this was all a dream. That she would wake up back in Delphine's house with her chest hollow from where her heart used to be.

His hand slid around her neck and held her head as their bodies moved together, the friction building their desires and bringing them closer and closer to the peak.

"Come with me," he urged.

She nodded, already more than halfway there. But at his words, it propelled her past the point of no return. All that was, all that mattered, was Marshall and how she felt in his arms.

And that's all she needed.

His grip tightened, and his face pinched as they both held back their pleasure as long as they could. Riley's breaths were loud, her body moving on its own as it careened toward the climax.

"Now," Marshall rasped.

Her head fell back as she gave in to the ecstasy. The pleasure slammed into her, cocooning her in light and decadence. The tremors ran through her body as she felt him shudder in her arms.

13

*U*tter contentment. That's what Marshall felt after making love to Riley. Their bodies were still joined, their breathing loud, when he realized for the first time in his life, he'd forgotten all about a condom.

As if Riley needed something else to worry about.

He watched as she lifted her face. He'd never seen anything so stunningly beautiful in his life. In every way, she was gorgeous, but now, with her face flushed and her lips swollen, she was exquisite.

They stared at each other, no words needed. Their bodies had said it all, and it was glorious.

She leaned forward and pressed her lips against his. Marshall hungrily kissed her, desire surging through him again. And he knew with the same certainty that the sun would rise in the east in the morning that he was falling for Riley.

Or perhaps he already had.

Hell, he didn't know. And honestly, he didn't care. At one time, he would've been afraid of loving someone, but it was different with Riley. *She* was different, unique. A woman all her own, and he loved everything about her.

From the living room through the closed door, Kane cleared his throat loudly, breaking their kiss. Riley's eyes widened as she smiled. Marshall couldn't believe he hadn't heard Kane walk back inside the house.

"Um...just thought I should let you two know that you might want to get dressed. Now," Kane said.

Riley rolled her eyes. "My cousins are on their way."

Marshall nodded. "Appears so."

"I'm not ready for this moment to end," she said softly.

He ran his hands down her face. "There will be others."

"Promise?"

"Promise."

It was the look in his eyes, the look that said he would move Heaven and Earth to be with her again that made her smile. She reluctantly rose and dressed.

"Riley."

She finished putting her hair atop her head and turned to Marshall. He looked so out of sorts that she frowned as she took a step toward him. "What is it?"

"I...we didn't use a condom."

There weren't too many men that would own up to such a thing, and it made her—

Her mind stopped because she'd nearly said love. How could she love him? She barely knew him. Yet, in the few days that she had, it seemed as if they had walked through Hell and clawed their way back again.

"It's all right," she assured him. "I get a shot every three months for that. Thankfully, I had one right before Delphine took me. Though I'm going to need to get that updated soon."

"Good. You have enough to deal with right now. You shouldn't have to worry about having children."

No sooner had the words reached her ears than she imagined

a little boy running around the Chiasson house in Lyons Point with dark waves and gray eyes.

"Right," she said, feeling a yearning she'd never experienced before.

"Riley!"

She winced at the sound of Solomon's booming voice. With one last look at Marshall, she walked out of the bedroom and was surrounded by Solomon, Minka, Myles, Addison, Court, and Skye.

It seemed impossible that she could forget her cousins and their women, and yet Delphine had wiped them from her memory. Just as the priestess had done with Riley's brothers and their loves.

To be held by her family was a wonderful thing. It made Riley realize how easily she could've lost it all. Thanks to Marshall, she was back where she belonged.

Well...sort of.

She pulled out of her cousins' arms and turned to the bedroom where Marshall was leaning against the doorframe, watching her. Though she couldn't explain how or why, she knew she should be with him. That that's where she belonged.

One side of his lips curved into a smile as if he too recognized what was going through her mind. She made her way to his side and looked up at him in wonder.

"Thank you," she said.

He quirked a brow. "For?"

"Coming to look for me."

Marshall straightened and put his hands on her arms, drawing her close. "Like your family, I knew you were here. And I didn't intend to leave without you."

"It worked."

"You can thank Kane for the idea of the symbols."

She turned so that she stood beside Marshall and looked at Kane and winked at him. "Thank you. All of you."

Myles glanced worriedly outside. "While I like this reunion, and I want to know everything that crazy bitch did to you, Riley, we need to prepare."

"He's right," Addison said as she put an arm around Myles. "Delphine will come for you again."

Minka snorted as she walked to stand before Riley. "My wards on you weren't strong enough last time, but I won't make that mistake again. Even if Delphine manages to take you again, she won't be able to hold you after I finish my spells."

Riley slid her gaze to Marshall as Minka began her magic. "It's nice to have a powerful witch as a friend."

"You have two," Solomon reminded her.

Riley nodded slowly. "I need to call my brothers."

"Already done," Court replied as he stood behind Skye, his hands on her shoulders.

Her eyes widened. "All of them?"

"Beau and Davena have already left with the others on their way," Solomon said once Minka was back by his side. "Since both Davena and Minka have gone up against Delphine before, we all figured it would be best to have both witches in the city."

Because of her, Riley realized. She was bringing the Chiassons and LaRues together—which was most likely exactly what Delphine wanted. What better way to wipe them all out?"

"What is it?" Marshall whispered as the others talked amongst themselves.

Riley leaned against him, loving his strength. He wasn't offended or intimidated by her independence or the fact that she was a hunter. Instead, he was like a wall around a fort, giving her courage and strength.

"This could be exactly what Delphine wants." She looked at

her cousins. They had found happiness—well, all except for Kane, but she wasn't giving up on him—and she didn't want to be the cause of destroying that.

Marshall leaned his head down so that he whispered in her ear. "That won't stop them from wanting to go against Delphine again."

"They survived three times already. The odds aren't in their favor. Then there are my brothers." She swallowed, emotion choking her as she imagined Delphine killing them.

"It won't happen," Marshall stated firmly.

But she knew it could. Easily. Delphine was that powerful. And while Delphine hadn't killed Riley's parents, the priestess had been responsible for murdering her aunt and uncle.

"We need the Moonstone pack," Court said.

Kane crossed his arms over his chest. "No."

"Though I don't want to call for them, we need them," Solomon said.

Myles shrugged. "The last we heard, Jaxon was still searching for Griffin."

To her horror, Riley then remembered Elin. "There was another woman with me. Delphine had her for much longer. She was—"

"Elin," Addison interrupted.

Riley blinked, her mind working to sort out how her cousins knew the name. She took a step back as more memories flooded back. "Oh, God. Griffin's sister."

Kane's arms dropped to his sides. "We need to get her from Delphine."

"You can't," Riley said and found herself reaching for Marshall's hand—and his strength.

"What happened?" Minka asked in a soft voice.

Riley squeezed Marshall's fingers. He remained composed

beside her, a rock upon which a steady foundation could be built. "George snapped her neck. We were going to leave together, but then Delphine told Elin that she was pregnant. It didn't help that I told Elin I saw her in some kind of a trance the night before where George had had sex with her."

"This isn't good," Minka said as she turned her head to look at Solomon. "At all."

Myles cut his eyes to her. "Meaning?"

"That is dark magic," Minka explained. Then she turned her gaze back to Riley. "I need to know everything about George."

For the next twenty minutes, Riley told them all that she knew about the man who'd followed her everywhere. She relayed every detail of her time with Delphine and everything that she saw and heard—including her last night with the priestess.

"I'm going to fucking rip her head from her body," Kane said with a low growl.

A muscle ticked in Marshall's jaw. "I know exactly how you feel."

"We need to be careful," Minka said as she glanced at the door.

Solomon looked at her and asked, "What do you mean?"

Minka's gaze swung from him to Riley. "George isn't just anyone. From the things you told us he said and did, that body is housing a spirit."

"And Delphine wouldn't just call up any spirit," Skye said.

Minka shook her head. "No, she wouldn't. That means, whoever is inside George is powerful. His fixation on Riley means that he's chosen who he wants as his."

"Over my dead body," Marshall declared.

Riley looked up at him, and in that moment, she knew that she was falling in love with him. And, somehow, that made facing what was to come easier.

Because she had someone as solid and strong-willed as Marshall by her side.

"We need to get Riley out of the city," Court said.

Minka stopped him before he could continue. "It won't do any good. George won't stop until he finds her."

"Then we take the bastard out," Marshall suggested.

Myles and Solomon exchanged a look before Solomon gave a nod of his head.

"Should we be doing this in the middle of the city?" Skye asked, her face filled with concern.

Addison nodded in agreement. "Exactly. Innocents could be killed."

"There's my place in the bayou," Minka offered.

But as her family talked, all Riley could think about was Marshall. She and her cousins had been born into this life. Minka, Skye, and Addison, as well as Olivia, Ava, Davena, and Ivy had all chosen it because of their love for the LaRues and Chiassons.

Riley faced Marshall and turned him to face her. "If you remain, she'll turn her focus on you."

"I'm not leaving you."

"You have a life," she said. "A career. You can get out now without her ever knowing your involvement. She won't touch you."

He gave a small shake of his head, his lips twisted. "That's where you're wrong, sweetheart because she's already touched my life by coming after you and your family."

"Then think of your future."

"I am."

Emotion welled within her so fast that she was choked by it. There was no denying that he meant *she* was his future when he said the words.

"Marshall," she began.

He put a finger to her lips. "I'm not leaving you. I can't. Don't you understand that? Can't you *feel* it?"

"Yes," she said breathlessly.

"Then you should know it'll take more than a Voodoo priestess to tear me away from your side."

Riley nodded.

And fell completely in love with Marshall Ducet.

14

*M*arshall stood before the living room window with all the lights off inside the house. Myles and Court had taken Addison and Skye to safety since neither of them had magic. Once the girls were set, the brothers planned to find Jaxon, who was leading the Moonstone pack until Griffin was found.

Riley sat behind him while Minka meditated in a bedroom. Marshall was aware of Riley's gaze on him, which made it difficult to keep an eye out for anyone because he kept thinking of how it felt to slide inside her.

"I'm scared."

Her confession hit him square in the chest. They were words he'd never thought to hear from her. Mostly because she was such a strong individual that he assumed she would keep it buried. And he loved that she was sharing it with him.

He turned to the side to look at her. "Any sane person would be. You've fought Delphine. You know what we're up against."

"My cousins and brothers worry about me," she said as she drew her legs up to her chest and rested her chin on her knees.

"I've made it my mission for them to believe that nothing frightens me."

Marshall nodded slowly. "I won't tell them."

She lowered her gaze to the floor. "So much could go terribly wrong."

"And it could go right. This isn't the first fight for your brothers or cousins. Or me."

Her eyes lifted to him. "It's the first time I've realized that I could lose absolutely everything in a heartbeat. Everyone I care about wants to fight her."

"Would you not do the same for anyone in your family?"

"Yes. Just as I would for you."

He glanced out the window to make sure no one was near. "I suspect this is why Vin fought so hard to keep you away."

"Now I understand how he and the others feel every night when they go hunting."

"This is different," Marshall said. "This isn't about hunting some monster or keeping the peace in New Orleans. This is about a priestess who has specifically targeted you and your family."

Riley rose from the sofa and walked to stand before him. "I can't lose them. Or you."

"You won't."

She shot him a dry look. "You can't promise such a thing."

"You're looking at your family through your eyes. Step back a moment and look through mine. Your brothers are a cohesive unit. They've been hunting together since they were kids. They know the bayous and every house in and around Lyons Point."

"But we're not there anymore."

He slid his fingers around hers. "No, we're in New Orleans where your cousins know every alley, street, and building around all districts while being just as unified as your brothers. Then you take those two organized groups and combine them with the Moonstone pack and the witches. All of which stood against Delphine before."

She released a long breath. "The way you say it gives me hope."

"Then cling to it."

"I can't just sit here while my family fights."

He grinned down at her. "I'd never suggest such a thing. I plan on being right beside you."

"And if I told you I wanted to run away from all of this?"

"I'd be with you."

He didn't say more because he knew what kind of woman Riley was, and the type of family she had. No matter how much she wanted to run, she would never do it. Her sense of duty to her family and the innocents she helped to protect drove her too hard. He understood that because it was part of what had made him want to become a cop.

Movement out of the corner of his eye had him whirling around and pulling his gun even as he shoved Riley behind him. He glared at the shape before him that stepped out of the shadows into the light that came through the window.

Vincent's gaze was steady, unflinching. Though no words passed the eldest Chiasson's lips, Marshall knew Vin had seen him and Riley together and most likely heard them talking.

Marshall lowered his arm. As soon as Riley saw her brother, she ran to him.

Vincent caught her in his arms and held her tight. "I've never been more worried in my life."

"I'm sorry."

"You're back now. That's all that matters," he said as he released her. Then he raised his gaze to Marshall. "You did what we couldn't. We owe you."

Marshall shook his head. "You owe me nothing."

"Where are the others?" Riley asked. "I want to see Christian, Beau, and Linc."

"They're with Solomon," Vin said.

As an only child, Marshall had always been fascinated with anyone who had siblings. He had seen the Chiasson brothers interact with one another on multiple occasions, but to watch them handle their sister as if she were a prized possession was fascinating.

Hell, even the way the LaRues treated Riley was interesting. While both families were in instant protective mode with her, the LaRues allowed Riley to be herself while her brothers tried in vain to keep her a little girl.

Despite the differences, there could never be any doubt that Riley was loved fiercely by all eight men—and the women who had come into the families.

Marshall turned to face the window and allow Vin and Riley some privacy. He tucked the gun back into the holster that he'd put on earlier and let his eyes move slowly over the area.

It wasn't long before Riley stood beside him. "Vin is staying close to the house and waiting on Beau to bring Davena. Apparently, she wanted Beau to drive her through the city a few times."

"She's getting reacquainted with the streets," Marshall said. "It's been a long time since Davena ran away from New Orleans and Delphine."

Riley drew in a deep breath. "There's something bothering you."

He glanced at her. "I find it intriguing to watch families, particularly how your brothers and cousins interact with you."

"Why?" she asked with a frown.

"I'm an only child. My parents tried for years to conceive without any luck. They decided to adopt and found me." He turned his head to her. "My birth mother was a twenty-year-old who got pregnant by her boyfriend before he was deployed— before either of them knew it. He was killed in action, and she decided she didn't want to raise a baby on her own."

"Oh, God. I'm so sorry," Riley said as her face lined with pity.

He shrugged. "My parents were amazing people. They loved me like their blood. I regret nothing."

"Except having siblings."

Marshall shrugged, even though it was true. "I would rather have had my parents."

"Have you tried to find your birth mother?"

"My parents gave me her name as well as my father's. I know where she is, but I've never wanted to see her. I don't hold any animosity towards her for what she did, but I also don't see a reason to have a connection with her."

Riley said nothing more. She merely wrapped an arm around his waist. He draped his arm over her shoulder and smiled. Who would've thought he would return to New Orleans for the very reason that he'd left?

Who would've thought that he would not only go looking for the supernatural but be prepared to fight it?

And who would've thought that he would find contentment during it all with a woman that made desire burn within him?

"If none of this had happened, how long do you think it would've been before we met?" she asked.

He thought about it a moment. "You'd be able to answer that better than I. How long before you returned home?"

"I didn't intend to for a very long time."

"Then I guess you have your answer."

She leaned her head against him. "When I think about not having you in my life, it makes what I went through with Delphine okay."

"I would've found you one way or another."

"I don't think anyone in my family can find love without some major event or someone's life being in danger."

Marshall's heart missed a beat. Had she just said love? Could she mean...was there even a chance that she felt as he did?

From the first time he'd seen Riley's photo at the Chiassons' he thought her beautiful, and had felt an inescapable, relentless need to know more about her. So he set about posing questions to the brothers until he began to formulate an idea of who Riley was.

It wasn't until he saw her at the Chiasson house that he knew his life would be tied to hers. He didn't know how or why or even when, but he'd known it as fact.

A truth he didn't try to ignore or discount.

Everything made sense when the weeks went by, and she couldn't be found. He'd known he needed to come look for her. Even if her brothers had not agreed, Marshall would've made the trip. Because he'd known he would find her. That somehow, something would lead him to her.

"Why does it feel as if I've known you my entire life?" she asked.

He rubbed his hand up and down her arm. "You mean, like we've already spent a lifetime or two together before?"

"And have found each other again," she said as she lifted her head to look at him.

"Yes."

She moved to stand in front of him, wrapping her arms around him as she did. "I'm going to tell you something I've never told anyone else before, but when I was a little girl of about five or six, I dreamed of a man and a woman deeply in love. I saw them fall in love, have a beautifully long, happy life, and die." She glanced down at his chest. "Even as a child, I knew the woman was me. All I needed to do was wait for the man who I belonged with."

"For me," he whispered before he kissed her.

Everything Riley had said resonated with him, striking a chord within his soul that he recognized. It explained so much. And how could he even think of discounting it now that he knew magic and supernatural creatures existed? Why not soul mates finding each other across lifetimes?

The kiss grew heated quickly, and he regrettably ended it because he knew they didn't have time to let pleasure overtake them again. He cupped her face, amazed at what he was feeling —and how deeply he felt it.

"Tell me we'll have more than one night together," Riley said.

"We will," he assured her. "One night isn't enough."

She grinned. "I'm not sure a million would be sufficient."

"Forever wouldn't be long enough."

"I don't think we should wait for Delphine to find me. I think we should go to her."

Marshall considered that for a moment. "It would allow us to set the time and location and use it to our advantage. And we could make her think she stumbled onto you."

Riley's eyes went wide. "I like the idea of tricking her. She'd be focused on me."

"And not see the rest of us coming."

"No doubt her followers are looking for me even now."

Marshall glanced toward the utility room. "Your clothes should be dry now."

"No time like the present to get things rolling, right?" she said with a forced smile.

He didn't want to let her out of his arms, but if they were going to have a shot at defeating Delphine, they had to take this chance. "Right."

She blew out a breath. "You better get Vin while I change."

Marshall turned and headed to the back door. If they were

lucky, no one had seen Beau and Davena yet. The other Chias-sons were coming in separately in secret so Delphine wouldn't know of their arrival.

And maybe, just maybe, if everything fell into place, then Marshall's plan would work—and Riley would be free of the priestess once and for all.

15

*H*er faith was being put to the test. Though it was her belief in herself and not her family—or Marshall.

Riley's heart raced, and her blood rushed in her ears as she looked out of the abandoned building into the darkness of the night. Her hands fisted as she wished she could reach over for Marshall. It would be so much easier to carry out her role in the trap if Marshall could stay beside her.

But she had to do this alone.

Which brought her back to her faith. She had fought vampires, ghosts, demons, and a number of other supernatural creatures, but none of them terrified her like Delphine did.

The fact that Riley had lived in the priestess's house for weeks as a *friend* sickened her. Actually, the very thought of Delphine made bile rise in Riley's throat.

So how was she going to stand there and not say the things she wanted to shout at Delphine? How was Riley supposed to act as if she still didn't have her memories?

And how did her brothers and cousins expect her not to try and kill the priestess herself?

The plan had come together quickly, and all of them had decided to act on it that night instead of waiting and allowing Delphine to discover that the Chiassons had come to the city. Now, her family was in their designated places with Davena and Minka each waiting to use their magic on Delphine and any of the other followers who got involved.

Riley tried not to glance over at Marshall, who stood beside her, because she might not be able to leave him if she did. She was glad that he would remain behind and take his position on the second floor as a sniper. Marshall's plan was solid, as was his confidence in her. That would get her through this.

"I won't be far," Marshall whispered.

God, how she wanted to touch him. "I know."

"I'll remain with you until you tell me you're ready. Everything is on your time. And you don't have to do any of it."

The more he spoke, the harder it was for her to keep her gaze straight ahead. But if she looked at him, if she touched him, she would never walk out there. "I do. Besides, this plan is the best one. She won't be expecting any of it."

He faced her and raked a hand through his dark, wavy hair. "I don't think you shou—"

She broke her rule and looked into his gray eyes while forcing a smile. He was struggling with the plan. And she knew he would stay with her if she asked it of him. That's how she knew it was time to get things moving. Because to remain with him, to continue living in fear of Delphine, allowed the priestess to win. And Riley couldn't accept that.

She started to walk away when Marshall grabbed her hand, halting her. Riley briefly closed her eyes before looking at him over her shoulder. He was the kind of man who would never falter, who would stand beside her in the very worst of times— like now—and during the best of times.

He was the kind of man who would love her deeply and

never let her down. The kind of guy who would always put her first. The kind of male who would love her from one life to the next.

She wouldn't let anyone break what she had found with Marshall, and that included Delphine. Riley was going to fight with everything she had because she wanted a life with Marshall more than she had ever wanted anything before.

"I love you," she said.

His eyes widened, but she pulled her hand out of his grasp and walked from the building before he could say anything. With her heart thumping wildly, Riley wrapped her arms around herself and kept her head down.

It wasn't an act. She was chilled, bone-deep, from walking away from Marshall. The anger and fear were so intertwined now that she could no longer tell one emotion from the other. And she didn't think it would get any better, at least until either Delphine was dead—or she was.

Riley stayed close to the building, making it look as if she were attempting to hide. Every once in a while, she would look over her shoulder or duck into an alleyway and peek around the corner.

She counted eleven of Delphine's followers, but no doubt there were others she didn't see. It wouldn't be long now before the priestess showed. And since this was the place her cousins had said was the best for battle, Riley walked slowly.

The streets were never deserted in New Orleans, but this district wasn't Delphine's. That made it significantly more dangerous because they were in the djinn's territory.

Riley had only encountered the djinn a few times, and quite frankly, they were scarier than the vampires. Still, the djinn were smart. They didn't kill everyone who walked their streets. Only a few individuals went missing from here. Most were taken from other parts of New Orleans.

As if sensing something in the air, people hurried away from her. Riley wanted to yell at anyone who remained. The idea of innocents getting brought into this war angered her, but she knew her family would make sure that those who were caught in the crossfire were protected.

Her thoughts drifted to the Moonstone pack. Tensions had run high since Griffin—the Alpha—and Solomon clashed over Minka. Yet, in the end, the pack had stood beside the LaRues to fight Delphine, even though Griffin had disappeared.

That battle was when Riley was taken. Not that she blamed her cousins. They'd all been fighting for their lives. It was no one's fault but hers that Delphine managed to get her hands on her. But she wondered if Delphine had gotten to Griffin, as well.

Riley shivered at the thought of how close Delphine had come to getting everything she wanted. While Riley wasn't entirely sure what the priestess and George had in mind for her, Riley knew it was probably very close to what they had done to Elin.

She cringed at the thought of her friend's death. If only Riley hadn't told her everything, perhaps she and Elin could've gotten away together. Maybe even now, Elin would be reunited with her brothers and her pack.

But thanks to Delphine and George, that was never to be. Just one more crime the priestess needed to pay for.

Riley was so deep in thought with her head down that she lurched to a stop when she saw the hem of a white skirt. Her head jerked up to find herself staring into Delphine's black eyes.

Riley took an unconscious step back while her gaze raked over Delphine's long, black braids hanging loose. The hatred that rose up in Riley was so powerful that she instantly fought against it so she wouldn't attack the priestess and ruin Marshall's plan.

Delphine could use that loathing against Riley, so she had to be careful.

"Hello, Riley," the priestess said in a pleasant tone.

Riley didn't answer. Simply took another step back.

Delphine's head cocked to the side. "Riley?"

"He killed Elin," she finally said.

Delphine's lips pressed together briefly. "I know."

"What are you going to do about it?" Riley demanded.

"I'm taking care of it, my way."

Riley hunched her shoulders. "I saw him snap her neck. He could do the same to me."

"He won't. George cares about you too much. Riley," Delphine said, taking a step closer. "You had me so worried. Where have you been?"

"Wandering the streets, trying to get away from George. I don't want him anywhere near me again."

"He's part of our family. It's going to take some time, but it'll all work out. Come to me, child."

Riley stood her ground. "I won't go back as long as George is there."

"He's family."

"And I'm not." Riley held Delphine's gaze. "I think it's best if I go, then."

"No!" Delphine bellowed when Riley turned to walk away.

Slowly, she turned back to the priestess. "You told me I was free to do as I wanted. I'm not a prisoner."

"You're returning with me," Delphine stated firmly.

Riley wrinkled her nose as she shook her head. "Actually, I'm not. While your magic worked for a while, your hold over me was broken days ago."

Delphine's gaze narrowed. "You stayed because you wanted to and because you had nowhere else to go."

"That's not entirely true, is it?" Riley asked. "Since my cousins live in the city. You know, the LaRues."

As soon as the words were out of her mouth, Solomon,

Myles, Kane, and Court stepped from their hiding places to surround Delphine. Even though the bar was being watched, they had snuck out of Gator Bait and made their way to Riley as soon as she walked out of the building.

"You're also well acquainted with my brothers," Riley continued.

Vin was the first to make an appearance behind Delphine. Then Christian, Beau, and finally Linc as they surrounded her.

Riley smiled as she watched Delphine's expression tighten. "Oh, and did I forget Minka and Davena?"

The two witches came to stand with the men.

"Is that all you have?" Delphine asked her. "I'm not without my own backup."

With a snap of her fingers, Delphine's disciples made a circle around Riley's family.

Riley smiled and raised her hand. Witches and members of the Moonstone pack—in werewolf form—filled the area.

"You've fought my brothers and Davena," Riley said. "You've even battled my cousins on several occasions, as well as Minka and our allies. But you've not faced all of us."

Delphine's chin lifted defiantly. "If you're trying to scare me, you're not doing a good job."

"I'm laying out the facts."

"Then let me lay one out for you," the priestess said. "I was able to kill two powerful LaRues to get them out of the way. I'm more than ready to wipe out not only your cousins but also your brothers and everyone who stands against me."

Riley yawned, covering her mouth as she did. Then she widened her eyes as she looked at Delphine. "I'm sorry. Did you say something? Because you keep reiterating the same shit."

"It looks like it's past the time for words," Delphine said.

In the back, one of the weres yelped loudly in pain. A second later, the sound was cut short. Riley didn't need to ask to know that the werewolf was dead. She kept her gaze on Delphine, using every ounce of control she possessed not to show any weakness.

She wanted to call for Marshall, to run to him and stand in his arms. But he was hiding, waiting for the final part of the plan. Except Riley wasn't sure she could make it to that finish line.

Someone who'd been helping her was now dead. She might not have known the werewolf personally, but it didn't matter. Delphine wasn't striking out at Riley's family—yet. But it was coming.

If Riley was already ready to break, she wouldn't survive once Delphine turned her brand of evil on the Chiassons or LaRues. Or Marshall.

Riley somehow stood her ground. Her knees knocked together, and her blood ran like ice through her veins. It was a horrible feeling, and she wanted it to end. Really, she was just ready for Delphine to die.

"Well?" Delphine asked. "Is this really what you want to do? Do you really want to go up against me and know that it'll mean the death of your family? Or will you walk away with me now? If you do, I allow them to live. I'll even take away your memories again. You were happy, Riley. Remember? You had no fear and no worries."

"But I wasn't me," Riley insisted. "Everyone here has chosen to rise up against you. We all know that this could be our last night on this earth, and we're all prepared to give our lives. If it means your death."

Delphine's eyes hardened. "Wrong choice."

Riley took a step back, and a second later, all hell broke loose.

rom his position on the second story of the building across the street, Marshall never took his eyes off Riley and Delphine. His gun was on his hip, but he held a rifle in hand, ready to lift and fire at the priestess.

All he could think about was Riley telling him that she loved him before walking away. He hadn't had time to respond, or even formulate a reply before she was gone. He'd wanted to pull her back, to tell her that he felt the same. Now, he had to wait until the battle was over.

Though he couldn't hear what Riley and Delphine were saying, he could tell by their expressions that things were heating up quickly.

Marshall lifted the rifle and peered through the scope. It was killing him not to be down there with the others, but he was Riley's backup. Because they all knew that Delphine was either going to either try and take Riley again—or kill her.

As long as he had breath in his body, that wouldn't happen.

He turned the gun and glanced through the scope at Lincoln, who was the closest to Riley. Linc was as still as a statue, a Bowie knife in each hand. While Lincoln never turned to look at Delphine's disciples behind him, he was very aware of them by the way he shifted just slightly in order to see them better.

Marshall gave a quick look at the rest of the Chiassons and LaRues before glancing back at Riley. Delphine's face was filled with fury, while Riley was smiling in triumph.

He lifted his head and glanced around at Delphine's followers. None had moved, but they were waiting for the priestess's decision. However, it was the werewolves who were crouched low and ready to spring that drew his attention.

Right about the time a were let out a shrill cry before everything went eerily quiet. Marshall knew the werewolf was dead.

So, this was how Delphine wanted to play it.

He once more gazed through the scope at Riley and Delphine. The grin Riley had worn slipped as they exchanged more words. Then she took a step back.

In that instant, Marshall moved his finger over the trigger. He was prepared to take the headshot on Delphine when the quiet was broken by a low growl before a melee the likes of which he'd never seen broke out.

He lost Riley in the chaos, and then he lost sight of Delphine. Lifting his head, he scanned the crowd of witches, werewolves, and humans for some sign of the priestess. Though he wanted to keep an eye on Riley, he knew her family would remain close.

It was Delphine that Marshall truly needed to find. As long as he could keep her in his sights, then Riley and the others had a fighting chance.

But everywhere he looked, there was no sign of her. It should be easy to pick out the white clothes in the darkness, but the crush of people clawing, slashing, hitting, and stabbing one another prevented him from seeing anything clearly.

He debated running up to the roof for a better view, but it

was time he couldn't take. Instead, he caught sight of one of Delphine's disciples coming up behind Kane. Without hesitation, he fired off a shot.

Kane whirled around and saw the dead man behind him. Then he gave a nod to Marshall before he returned to the fighting.

Marshall continued looking for Riley and Delphine while picking off more and more of the enemy. Delphine and her people were seriously outnumbered, yet that didn't seem to factor in their decision to fight.

All Marshall could be thankful for was that this battle playing out in the middle of the streets of New Orleans hadn't drawn any policeman, nor had any innocents been affected. Yet.

But it was only a matter of time.

Riley winced as she fell back and slammed against the side of a building. She saw a fist come at her, and she quickly ducked. When she straightened to deliver her own blow, Beau had already taken down her opponent.

"Where's Delphine?" Beau asked.

She shrugged. "I haven't seen her since the fight began. One minute she was in front of me, and the next, she was gone."

"That's not good," he murmured as he pivoted to continue fighting.

Riley looked around for someone to battle, but everyone was already matched up. Thankfully, more of Delphine's followers lay dead than anyone in her group.

The sound of a rifle firing had her lifting her gaze to the window where Marshall was stationed. She hoped that he'd found Delphine and could end all of this with literally one bullet. But he fired two more rounds in quick succession in various places.

She saw one of the disciples fall and knew that Marshall was helping in the battle while looking for Delphine. He was their secret weapon, though with every bullet he fired, he drew attention to himself.

Riley felt the hairs on the back of her neck lift. She looked around, seeking the source, and found George standing off to the side, watching her. Then his gaze slid to Marshall's position before George turned on his heel.

She lost him as the crowd shifted, blocking her view. She pushed against a witch while trying to hurry after George, but it felt as if, suddenly, everyone was closing in around her.

"Marshall!" she yelled.

Her cry was swallowed by the sounds of battle.

The harder she tried to move through the throng of people, the less distance she was able to achieve. She kept glancing up at the window. Every time Marshall fired the gun, relief filled her.

She was finally able to push through the last of the group and stumbled out onto the deserted street. Her gaze jerked to the window where Marshall's rifle barrel no longer poked out.

Riley ran toward the building, praying with each step that he wouldn't be hurt in any way. She reached the door and threw it open to run inside when Kane suddenly appeared beside her.

His hand on her arm halted her. "What?"

"Marshall."

That's all that was needed. Her cousin gave her a nod and rushed inside. He reached the stairs first, taking them three at a time while she followed as fast as she could.

The battle raged on outside, the sounds dimmed by the walls of the structure. But it was the silence from above that scared her.

They reached the top of the landing, and Kane motioned to

her that he was going to come in another way. Riley didn't care. She just wanted to find Marshall.

Her heart was in her throat when she ran to the doorway and looked inside to find George and Marshall glaring at each other. Riley glanced at Marshall, but she kept her full attention on George.

"You don't belong up here," she told George.

He turned his cold, dark eyes to her. "And you do?"

"Leave."

"I'm here for you."

Riley could feel the tension and anger rolling off Marshall. If George were just a man, she would let Marshall take him down, but George was something much more. And that's what made her leery of him.

"I'm not going anywhere with you or Delphine," Riley stated.

George cut his eyes to Marshall. "Because of him."

"Because I don't want to be with you. Because I'm not a possession. I'm a woman who has the right to choose, and I choose my family."

George turned his head back to her. "I can give you everything. Power, wealth, status, and the ability to rule all of New Orleans."

Out of the corner of her eye, she saw Marshall frown. Riley shrugged. "First, I don't care about any of that. Second, Delphine wants to run New Orleans."

"I can give it to you."

The way he said it sent a chill of foreboding down Riley's spine. She spotted Kane coming up behind George, but she wasn't ready for his attack yet. Moving the fingers of her right hand, she waved Kane off for the moment.

"What do you mean you can give it to me?" Riley asked.

George smiled, his gaze locked on her. "I can give you anything you want. All you have to do is come with me."

"Tell me how you can do what you claim."

He waved his hand around him and glanced out the window. "Once, a very long time ago, I ran New Orleans. Nothing went on in this city that I didn't approve of. My magic was unbeatable. I was the strongest around. And everyone knew it."

"But you died," she said before Marshall could.

George lifted one shoulder in a shrug. "I was betrayed by those who wanted someone else in power."

"Who?" she asked.

"A family. The LaRues came to the city and began driving out the worst of the supernatural. They were chosen to regulate the city. And their first order of business was to get rid of me."

She took a step closer to George even as Marshall whispered her name, and Kane glowered. "Why do you want me?"

"Because only my spirit is here. I control this body since Delphine summoned me, but I want more. I want to take my place at the head of this city once again. And you can give that to me."

"How?"

"A blood sacrifice. And a child."

She grimaced. "You mean you'll be reborn?"

"No. The sacrifice will make sure that I can never be removed from this body."

Even though she knew she didn't want to know the answer, she asked, "And the child?"

"We'll create a dynasty so strong that no one will ever be able to destroy it."

She shook her head. "LaRue blood runs in me through my family. I'm your enemy."

"You can see it that way, or you can be my ally. I'll spare

your family—all of them—but they must leave New Orleans forever."

Riley swallowed. "Who is to be the sacrifice?"

"Delphine, of course."

Riley could barely believe his response. But she didn't have time to answer as there was a loud shriek that made Riley bend at the waist and cover her ears with her hands.

She looked over to find Delphine striding into the room with her gaze full of vengeance and death. Another blood-curdling scream filled the air as the priestess sent George flying backwards.

He slammed into the wall and dropped to the floor without an ounce of pain showing. He got to his feet and blinked as if he'd suspected such a show.

Marshall was suddenly at Riley's side. He took her hand and was leading her out when she gasped as an arm wrapped around her waist and jerked her back out of Marshall's grip. He spun around at the same time Kane made himself known.

The five of them stared at each other in silence. And then Riley felt as if something were tightening around her throat. She clawed at her neck and struggled to breathe, gasping for air.

"Delphine," George warned.

Riley was unceremoniously dropped. She fell to the floor with her mouth open wide and her lungs burning for breath. Marshall was immediately at her side, but there was nothing he could do.

The corners of her vision began to swim as black dots appeared. Riley knew she was dying. Marshall looked on help-lessly as Kane made to attack Delphine. Except George beat him to it.

George was fast and strong, and he moved as if he knew what Delphine was thinking. It allowed him to get close and slam her head against the wall.

Riley choked as the pressure on her neck vanished, and she dragged in mouthfuls of precious air. As her lungs filled, the rushing in her ears ceased so she could hear again.

"I love you. I love you. I love you," Marshall repeated over and over again.

She looked up at him and smiled.

17

*I*f they remained, they were going to die. Marshall pulled Riley to her feet as George turned to them. Delphine pushed herself up onto her hands and knees and slowly turned her head to George.

The rage in the priestess's eyes warned of retribution and violence. And Marshall didn't want Riley anywhere near such happenings. She'd already been through too much already.

And he'd come so very close to losing her.

Delphine used the wall to climb to her feet. George turned back to her while Kane kept his gaze locked on the priestess. Both stood against Delphine, but even then, Marshall wasn't sure who would come out the victor.

For the moment, Kane and George were on the same side, but how long would that last once they took down Delphine? Probably no more than a few seconds before George realized that he wasn't going to get Riley, and then he would attack all of them.

"Fuck," Marshall murmured.

Riley was still wobbly on her feet, but with each second, she gained strength. He glanced behind him out the window to see that the battle was still raging, but there were few of Delphine's followers left standing.

"How dare you," Delphine said to George through clenched teeth.

He smiled, but it was cold, unfriendly. "You shouldn't be surprised."

"We were supposed to work together," she stated.

"I would have said anything to come back. Now that I'm here, I'm going after what I want."

Marshall's gut clenched when George turned his head and looked right at Riley.

"Over my fucking dead body," Kane declared.

George's black eyes met the werewolf's. "That can be arranged."

"Not if I kill you," Delphine said.

Riley leaned close to Marshall and whispered, "Get ready."

Marshall debated turning and getting his rifle. Though he would be better served with his pistol—if he could get a shot off.

The tension ratcheted up so high, the air fairly vibrated with it. George and Delphine stared at each other, while Kane's eyes moved from one to the other. And all three were ready for anything.

Riley took Marshall's hand. He palmed his gun with the other and pulled it from the holster. While he wanted to kill Delphine, his attention was on George. With him and Kane, surely they could eliminate at least one of their enemies this night.

Marshall's gaze darted to the two doorways. To get to either meant getting near George and Delphine. The two windows behind him were out of the question since it was a straight drop to the pavement below.

If only the building had a balcony, then that would give them several options. But there was no use wanting something that wasn't there.

"Get to your brothers," he whispered.

Riley shot him a flat look that said she wasn't going anywhere.

The sound of Delphine's laughter sent a chill down Marshall's spine. Even Kane was affected by the maniacal cackle. The only one who didn't seem bothered was George.

He tilted his head to the side and calmly said, "Let's get on with this, shall we?"

In the next instant, Delphine launched her attack.

Marshall grabbed Riley and dove to the side as George slammed into the wall where they had been standing. Marshall briefly met Riley's gaze before they jumped to their feet.

Kane went after Delphine, but he only got a few steps before she had him hanging in midair. Then her head snapped to George as he got to his feet and dusted himself off.

It was all casual right up until he lifted his gaze to Delphine. Marshall saw the evil within the man then, the malevolent spirit that was prepared to do anything to get what he wanted.

And right now, he wanted Delphine dead.

George moved so quickly that Marshall couldn't keep up with him. One moment Delphine was standing, and the next, she was gone. Kane dropped to his knees as he fell to the floor. And then George turned his attention to Riley.

Marshall shook his head and tried to move her behind him. "She doesn't want to go with you."

"I can give her everything you can't," George said.

Then, without missing a beat, George looked over his shoulder at Kane and used magic to lift Kane and toss him out of the room.

"As I was saying," George replied once his attention was back on Marshall. "I'm going to give you one chance to step away from what's mine. If you don't, I'll kill you."

Riley gave a loud snort. "Yours? I'm not yours. I never was, and I *never* will be."

"What a pity," George said in a soft voice. "I'd hoped you would come willingly. I didn't want to force you, but I'm prepared to do whatever is necessary."

All the fear that had been pressing against Marshall from the moment they put this plan into motion evaporated. He'd been in this position countless times before—only this was his first time where everything directly connected to him.

He wasn't going to watch George take Riley away. Nor would he stand aside and give in to George's demands. While Marshall might not be a werewolf or have the skills of a lifelong supernatural hunter, he did know bad guys.

And he was in love with Riley.

All of that meant one thing—he had to give Riley time to get to her brothers and cousins. With them, she had a chance of fighting against George.

He didn't think about all the dreams that had flooded his mind over the past few hours of having a life with Riley. Or of a love so deep and profound, one that he'd never expected to find.

If all he was meant to have were these few precious hours with Riley, then he would take them with a smile, knowing that he was about to ensure that she continued to live. That the world would be a brighter, happier place with her in it.

Marshall pulled her behind him as he took a step back and to the side. He was trying to inch closer to the door, but by George's raised brow, the bastard knew exactly what Marshall was attempting.

"You've chosen poorly," George said and lifted his hands.

Marshall turned and pressed Riley against the wall, shielding her with his body as he waited for whatever magic George was about to unleash on them.

Instead, a scream of rage rent air. Marshall's gaze cut to the doorway to see Delphine stride into the room with her lips peeled back in a snarl as she advanced on George.

The building began to shake from the force of the magic between Delphine and George. The two were utterly focused on each other. Or so Marshall thought. Just as he was about to lead Riley to the door, Marshall felt himself being lifted and tossed against the far wall.

He hit the ground with a thud, his head slamming against the floor. Pain exploded through him even as he fought to stay conscious.

"Marshall."

He heard the worry in Riley's voice as she kneeled beside him, her hands on him as she helped him sit up. "You need to leave," he said, holding a hand to his throbbing head.

"Not without you."

Of course, she'd be stubborn. Not that he could find fault in her words. He'd do the same in her position.

"Come on," she said as she slung his left arm around her shoulders.

He tightened his grip on his gun even as he struggled to his feet. His gaze was riveted on George and Delphine, but now he realized that while it appeared George was focused on the priestess, the bastard was always aware of where Riley was.

"What are you thinking?" Riley whispered.

There was no way they were getting to the door. It would be easier to get out that way, plus they could check on Kane. But Marshall knew they couldn't get close to either of the two doorways. George had positioned himself in such a way that they would have to get near him in order to get out.

The only other option was the windows.

"Are you afraid of heights?" he asked.

Riley shook her head. "Windows, then?"

"I'm afraid so."

"And Kane?"

"We'll come back."

She glanced out the door. "Yes, we will."

Marshall jerked his chin to the nearest window. "Get it open. I'll watch the two psychopaths."

As she worked to open the old windows that had been painted shut, the ceiling began to crumble and fall from the magic being thrown between George and Delphine. Marshall raised his gun and sighted down the barrel. The moment he got a shot, he fired at George.

Except the asshole moved at the last minute, causing the bullet to lodge in the wall. And then George turned his fury on Marshall.

His pistol heated in his hand, causing his skin to smoke. Marshall fired off two more shots, both going wide before he had no choice but to drop the weapon. The only thing that kept George from coming straight for Marshall was Delphine, who hadn't let up her assault.

There was a loud bellow followed by Kane leaping into the room. His eyes were bright yellow as he rushed George. When Kane tackled him to the ground, Delphine came in for the kill.

"Get out!" Kane bellowed to Marshall.

He didn't hesitate. He grabbed Riley's hand and ran to the door. Large chunks of the ceiling fell all around them. The stairs were separating from the floor that swayed beneath their feet.

Marshall never slowed. His hold on Riley was tight as they ran down the stairs toward the doors. No sooner had they sped from the stairs than they crumbled behind them, filling the air with a dust cloud that enveloped them.

"Kane!" Riley screamed.

Marshall paused long enough to wrap his arms around her waist and haul her against him when she tried to go back for her cousin. He glanced up and saw the massive cracks in the ceiling. The entire building was about to come down.

He barreled through the doors when he heard the loud crack that split the air. The sight of friendly faces had relief pouring through him.

Riley was pulled from his arms and engulfed in her brothers', but her gaze never left the building.

"Where's Kane?" Court asked.

Myles came to stand beside his brought. "Listen."

The street quieted as everyone raised their gazes to the second floor where the sounds of growls could be heard over George's bellows and Delphine's screeches.

Solomon pushed past his brothers and started toward the building even as Kane released a howl. Solomon paused, glancing upward, before continuing on. Right before he reached the doors, the building gave a great yawning noise before collapsing in on itself.

Marshall reached for Riley. She slammed into his arms before he turned and shielded her from the flying debris of the building. It felt like an eternity before the dust began to settle. Marshall heard the approaching sirens and straightened.

He glanced at everyone before his gaze landed on Riley. "All of you need to leave. Now."

"No," she said.

Solomon nodded. "He's right. We should all go."

"What about Kane?" Christian asked.

Court raked a hand through his hair, dislodging dirt. "There's a very good chance he got away. His howl told us that."

"We won't do him any good in jail," Myles said.

Beau held out his hand for Davena as she and Minka walked up. "Then let's head out."

The others began to walk away, but Riley stayed with Marshall. "You should go with him," he said.

She raised her blue eyes to his. "My place is by your side."

"They'll want to question you," he warned.

She shrugged. "It won't be the first time."

Marshall wrapped an arm around her shoulders and waited for the first responders to arrive. The sky was turning a soft gray with the first hint of dawn.

"So many dead," she murmured.

He glanced at her. "But we're not."

"Do you think we could be lucky enough to have both Delphine and George dead?"

"It's a possibility."

She blew out a breath. "Kane can't be gone."

Their talking ceased as the first police cruiser arrived, followed by fire trucks and an ambulance. Soon, the entire area was bathed in red and blue flashing lights.

Just as Marshall had known, detectives repeatedly questioned them while others searched through the rubble of the building for bodies. The story he and Riley told of walking through the streets on a date and coming across a massive gang fight seemed to be accepted. Though no one had an explanation for why the building came down.

The soft light of dawn was soon replaced by the bright light of day. Riley was wrapped in a blanket in the back of an ambulance as paramedics checked her over while she drank a cup of coffee.

Someone said Marshall's name. He turned his head to find John Gallagher, who he had known well before leaving the city. Marshall's eyes immediately went to the badge hanging around his neck.

"Captain now, huh? I'm not surprised. Congrats," Marshall said.

John gave a nod. "Thanks. Now, how about you tell me what really happened."

"I don't know what you mean."

"Bullshit. You always pretended you didn't know about the supernatural in the city, but I knew you did. You were too careful."

Marshall studied John a long minute. "You plan on putting this in your report?"

"Hell no," he said with his face scrunched up. "I'd like to continue on my career path. This will be for my information only."

Marshall glanced at Riley to find her watching him. He returned his attention to John and took a deep breath before condensing the story for his old friend.

"Fuck me," the captain said and ran a hand down his face.

Marshall shrugged one shoulder. "Aptly put."

"We've got a body!" someone shouted from the remains of the building.

Marshall held his breath, praying it wasn't Kane. Riley came to stand beside him and took his hand in hers. Both anxiously waited for the men to clear the debris from the body and pull him out.

"It's George," Riley said as soon as they got a glimpse of him.

Marshall winced when they saw the odd angle of George's neck, but it was the gaping wound that showed Kane's ferocity.

Even with fatigue weighing heavily upon both Marshall and Riley, they remained for hours until the authorities deemed that no other bodies could be found.

As one, he and Riley turned and walked from the scene arm-in-arm. They were quiet, letting the horror of the night fade with each step they took.

They were a few blocks from Gator Bait when Riley stopped and faced him. Marshall smoothed his hands down either side of her face. Her cheeks were smudged with dirt, and he was sure he didn't look any better.

"I was almost positive I was going to die last night," she said.

He nodded slowly. "I feared you would, as well."

"It's why I left so quickly after telling you my feelings. I knew if you said anything that I'd never walk out those doors."

Marshall pulled her against him and wrapped his arms around her as he kissed the top of her head. If he lived a hundred years, he would never forget what it felt like to help-lessly hold her as Delphine choked her to death.

"I love you," he said. "I'd stand beside you every day battling evil if it meant I got to hold you in my arms."

She lifted her head and smiled at him. "Life with me isn't going to be easy. I've got four interfering brothers and four nosy cousins."

"I've always wanted a big family."

"I'm afraid you've bitten off more than you can chew," she teased.

He glanced to the side, twisting his lips. "I'll have you beside me through it all."

"Always."

Neither could stop smiling as they walked into the bar. The mood was subdued as everyone waited for word about Kane, but Marshall didn't have long before he was pulled from Riley and surrounded by the Chiassons and LaRues.

"I love her," he told them.

Vin's smile was huge. "And we wholeheartedly approve."

"To Marshall and Riley," Beau said as he held up his beer.

As everyone toasted, Marshall looked beyond the men to find Riley at the bar with the women. Their gazes met. Love and warmth spread through him.

Against all the odds, he'd found the one woman who was meant to be his.

And the one person who he was meant for.

Life couldn't get any better.

EPILOGUE

Three weeks later...

*R*iley wiped at a tear that escaped and adjusted the bouquet of flowers in her hand. She stood at the front of the church as a bridesmaid, watching Vin and Olivia say their vows. Beside her, Ava had stopped all attempts to hold back her tears.

Looking out over the pews, Riley spotted Christian and Davena, and Beau and Ivy as well as Solomon, Minka, Myles, Addison, Court, and Skye. The absence of Kane was felt by all, but each of them held onto hope that he was still alive.

Riley glanced at Vin, who was grinning like a fool at Olivia. Lincoln, who was best man, only had eyes for Ava, and Riley suspected that they were thinking of their own wedding since they had gotten engaged after they all returned from New Orleans.

But it was the man on the other side of Linc who drew Riley's attention. Marshall Ducet was her everything. She loved him with her whole heart.

They shared a secret smile. It had killed Riley not to put on the ring this morning after he proposed the previous night, but both had agreed that the day was for Olivia and Vin. There would be time enough later to celebrate their engagement.

As a matter of fact, there would be a lot of celebrating. Along with Linc and Ava, both Beau and Christian had proposed, which meant Davena and Ivy would officially become her sisters soon, as well.

Riley cut her gaze to Minka, who was staring up at Solomon with so much love that it made Riley smile. She spotted the sparkler on Minka's left hand, but she wasn't surprised. Solomon and Minka belonged together, and they weren't going to wait.

Riley didn't think it would be much longer before Court and Skye were also engaged. Yet there would be no more weddings until they learned what had become of Kane. And Riley planned to be right there with them searching.

Everyone erupted in applause and cheers when the priest told Vin that he could kiss his bride. And then they were walking back down the aisle. Riley smiled as she took Marshall's arm.

"Your thoughts give you away," he said with a wink.

She grinned at him. "Is it that obvious?"

"Only to me," he admitted.

Once they were out of the church, he took her in his arms and pressed her against the side of the building before kissing her deeply. When he lifted his head, she was clinging to him breathlessly.

"Not fair," she said.

"It's going to be us up there soon."

"And I can't wait."

Marshall moaned as he kissed her again. "Me, either."

They broke apart and hurried after the others to begin the reception where the entire town was invited. The celebration was amazing, but Kane's absence was glaring.

"We'll find him," Marshall said. "Just as I found you. But that's for tomorrow. Tonight, we party."

She laughed as he led her out onto the dance floor. Marshall was her future and everything she held dear. Nothing and no one would ever tear them apart—not even death.

THANK YOU!

Thank you for reading *Wild Rapture*. I hope you enjoyed it! I love getting to step back into this paranormal world.

If you liked this book – or any of my other releases – please consider rating the book at the online retailer of your choice. Your ratings and reviews help other readers find new favorites, and of course there is no better or more appreciated support for an author than word of mouth recommendations from happy readers. Thanks again for your interest in my books!

Donna Grant
www.DonnaGrant.com

Look for the first book in my Heart of Texas series –
THE CHRISTMAS COWBOY HERO
Coming October 31, 2017!

Clearview, Texas
Three weeks before Christmas

This shit couldn't be happening. Abby Harper's heart thumped against her ribs as she turned into the parking lot of the sheriff's department. She parked and opened her car door, only to have her keys drop from her shaking hands. It took her three tries to pick them up because she couldn't get her fingers to listen to what her brain was telling them.

Along with the fact that her brother had been arrested, her mind couldn't stop thinking about the money she was losing for leaving her job early to find out what happened. Which meant that there was a real possibility that she would have to choose between paying for electricity or groceries next week.

She hunkered into her coat, bracing against a blast of cold air as she hurried to the door of the building. As soon as she was inside, the heat engulfed her.

Coming through the speakers overhead was the old Willie Nelson and Waylon Jennings song *Momma, Don't Let Your Babies Grow Up to be Cowboys.*

The irony wasn't lost on her. The problem was, she'd done everything she could. But Clearview was in cattle country. That meant there were cowboys everywhere—as well as rodeos that happened too frequently to even count.

Abby licked her lips and walked up to the counter and the glass window. A man in a uniform slid back the pane and raised his blond brows in question. His look told her he didn't care what had brought her there or what sad story she might have.

"Hi," she said, her voice squeaking. Abby cleared her throat and tried again. "Hi. I'm here about Brice Harper."

"You don't look old enough to be his mother," the man stated as he reached for a file.

After all these years, Abby should've been used to such a response. But she didn't think a person ever got used to such things.

She forced a half smile. "I'm his sister, but also his legal guardian."

"And your parents?"

If it had been anyone but a sheriff's deputy, Abby would've told them it was none of their business.

"Dad died years ago, and our mother ran off. But not before she gave me legal guardianship of my brothers."

The man's dark eyes widened. "You have another brother?"

"Yes."

As if she needed another reminder that she was failing at raising her siblings.

"Through that door," the deputy said as he pointed to his left.

A loud beep sounded, and Abby dashed to open the door. She walked through it to find another police officer waiting for her. Despite Brice's reckless nature and the rowdy crowd he hung with, this was her first time at a police station.

And, quite frankly, she prayed it was her last.

Nothing could prepare anyone for what awaited them once they entered. The plain white walls, thick doors, locks, and cameras everywhere made her feel as if the building were closing in on her. And that didn't even take into account all the deputies watching her as she walked past.

She wasn't sure if being taken back to see Brice was a good

thing or not. Wasn't there supposed to be something about bail? Not that she could pay it.

Her thoughts came to a halt when the deputy stopped by a door and opened it as he stepped aside. Abby glanced inside the room before she looked at him. He jerked his chin toward the door.

She hesitantly stepped to the entrance. Her gaze landed on a familiar figure, and relief swamped her. "Danny."

"Hi, Abby," he said as he rose from his seat at the table in the middle of the room.

His kind, hazel eyes crinkled at the corners with his smile. He walked to her then and guided her to the table. All her apprehension vanished. Not even the fact that he also wore a sheriff's deputy uniform bothered her. Because she'd known Danny Oldman since they were in grade school.

He'd run with the popular crowd at school because he'd been one of the stars of the football team, but Danny never forgot that he'd grown up in the wrong part of town—next door to her.

"I'm so glad you're here," she said.

His smile slipped a little. "What Brice did is serious, Abby."

She pulled out the chair, the metal scraping on the floor like a screech, and sat. "No one has told me anything. Brice refused to speak of it. He just told me to come."

"Perhaps you should be more firm with him."

The deep voice sent a shiver through her. She hadn't realized anyone else was in the room. Abby looked over her shoulder to see a tall, lean man push away from the corner and walk toward her.

His black Stetson was pulled low over his face, but she got a glimpse of a clean-shaven jaw, square chin, and wide, thin lips. It wasn't until he stopped across the table from her and flattened his hands on the surface that she remembered to breathe.

"Abby," Danny said. "This is Clayton East. Clayton, Abby Harper."

It was a good thing she was already sitting because Abby was sure her legs wouldn't have held her. Everyone knew the Easts. Their ranch was the largest in the county. The family was known to be generous and welcoming, but that wasn't the vibe she got from Clayton at the moment.

Then it hit her. Whatever Brice had done involved the East Ranch. Of all the people for her brother to piss off, it had to be them. There was no way she could compete with their wealth or influence. In other words, her family was screwed ten ways from Sunday.

Clayton lifted his head, pushing his hat back with a finger. She glimpsed strands of blond hair beneath the hat. Her gaze clashed with pale green eyes that impaled her with a steely look. No matter what she did, she couldn't look away. She'd never seen so much bottled anger or anguish in someone's stare before.

It stunned her. And she suspected it had nothing to do with her brother or the ranch but something else entirely. She wondered what it could be.

"No," she said.

What should've been internal dialogue came out. Clayton's blond brows snapped together in confusion. She glanced at Danny, hoping that her outburst would be ignored. It wasn't as if Clayton needed to know that her history with men was . . . well, it was best left forgotten.

When she looked back at Clayton, she was arrested by his rugged features. He wasn't just handsome. He was gorgeous. Skin tanned a deep brown from the sun only highlighted his eyes more. His angular features shouldn't be appealing, but they were oh, so attractive.

She decided to look away from his face to gather herself but realized that was a mistake when her gaze dropped to the denim shirt that hugged his wide, thick shoulders. The sleeves were rolled up to his forearms, showcasing the edge of a tattoo that she almost asked to see.

Abby leaned back in her chair, which allowed her to get a better glimpse of Clayton East's lower half. Tan-colored denim hung low on his trim hips and encased his long legs.

He was every inch the cowboy, and yet the vibe he gave off said he wasn't entirely comfortable in such attire. Which couldn't be right. He'd been raised on the ranch. If anyone could wear such clothes with authority, it was Clayton East.

Danny cleared his throat loudly. Her gaze darted to him, and she saw his pointed look. Wanting to kick herself, Abby drew in a deep breath. Just as she was about to start talking, Clayton spoke.

"Cattle rustling is a serious offense."

Abby's purse dropped from her hand to the floor. She couldn't have heard right. "Cattle rustling?"

"We picked up Brice trying to load cattle with the East brand on them into a trailer," Danny said. "Those with him ran off."

She was going to be sick. Abby glanced around for a garbage can. This couldn't be happening. Brice was a little reckless, but weren't most sixteen-year-olds?

Though she knew that for the lie it was. She'd known from the moment their mother walked out on them that it would be a miracle if Brice graduated high school. He acted out, which was his way of dealing with things.

"I . . . I . . . ," She shook her head.

What did one say in response to such a statement? Sorry? I don't know what's wrong with him?

Danny propped himself on the edge of the table and looked down at her, his hazel eyes filled with concern. "You should've come to me if Brice was out of control."

"He hasn't been, though," she argued. And that wasn't a lie. "Brice's grades have improved, and he's really straightened up."

Danny blew out a long breath. "Is there anyone new he's been hanging around with?"

"No," she assured him. "Not that I've seen."

After the last incident when Brice was about to enter a house that his friends had broken into, he'd sworn he wouldn't get into any more trouble. Abby truly believed that the brush with the law had set him straight.

Her heart sank as she realized that her brother could very well go to jail. She knew she was a poor substitute for their mother, but she'd done the best she could.

"What happens now?" she asked, racking her brain to come up with memories of past shows she'd seen to indicate what would happen next. "Is there a bail hearing or something?"

"That depends on Clayton."

Just what she needed.

But Abby was willing to do anything for her brothers. She sat up straight and looked Clayton in the eye. "My brother is young and stupid. I'm not making excuses for him, but he's had a hard time since our mother left. I'm doing everything I can to—"

"You're raising him?"

She halted at his interruption before nodding. "Both Brice and Caleb."

He stared at her for a long, silent minute.

Abby wasn't too proud to beg. And she'd even get on her knees if that was what it took. "Please don't press charges. I'll pay back whatever it is you've lost with the theft."

"Abby," Danny said in a harsh whisper.

"Is that so?" Clayton asked as he crossed his arms over his chest. "You're really going to repay my family?"

Abby looked between Clayton and Danny before returning

her gaze to Clayton and nodding. Her throat clogged because she knew the amount would be enormous, but if it meant her brother wouldn't go to jail, she'd gladly pay it.

"There were a hundred cows stolen. Thirty of them were recovered when your brother was arrested, which leaves seventy unaccounted for. Let's round it to $2000 each. That's $140,000. Not to mention that each of them is about to calf. Each calf will go for a minimum of $500 each. That's an additional $35,000."

Oh, God. She would be paying for the rest of her life. And she was fairly certain Clayton wanted the payment now. How in the world was she ever going to come up with that kind of money?

But Clayton East wasn't finished. He had yet to deliver the killing blow.

"Then there's Cochise, one of our prized bulls. He's worth $100,000."

She put a hand over her mouth as her stomach rebelled. She really was going to be sick, and at the moment, the idea of vomiting on Clayton East sounded tempting.

There was no way she could come up with $275, much less $275,000. Worse, Clayton knew it. It was written all over his face.

Danny rose to his feet and stood at the end of the table. "Abby, you need to get Brice to tell you where the rest of the cattle are."

The words barely penetrated her mind. She stared at the metal table, her mind blank. Usually, she was able to think up some way to get her brothers out of whatever mess they'd gotten into—and there had been some real doozies.

She'd toiled through various jobs until she landed a position at the CPA company where she was currently employed. Despite the fact that she worked sixty hours a week, they wouldn't put her on salary because that would mean they'd have to give her health insurance.

Even with those hours and every cent she scraped together, it still didn't cover their monthly bills. But the one thing she'd promised her brothers was that she would take care of them.

And she had.

Up until today.

She scooped up her purse and stood before facing Danny. "I'd like to see my brother now."

It took everything within her to walk out of the room without giving the high and mighty Clayton East a piece of her mind.

NEVER MISS A NEW BOOK

FROM DONNA GRANT!

Sign up for Donna's newsletter!
http://eepurl.com/bRI9nL

Be the first to get notified of new releases and be eligible for special subscribers-only exclusive content and giveaways.
Sign up today!

ABOUT THE AUTHOR

New York Times and *USA Today* bestselling author Donna Grant has been praised for her "totally addictive" and "unique and sensual" stories. She's written more than seventy novels spanning multiple genres of romance including the bestselling Dark King stories. Her acclaimed series, Dark Warriors, feature a thrilling combination of Druids, primeval gods, and immortal Highlanders who are dark, dangerous, and irresistible. She lives with two children, a dog, and three cats in Texas.

Connect with Donna online:
www.DonnaGrant.com

www.facebook.com/AuthorDonnaGrant
www.twitter.com/donna_grant
www.goodreads.com/donna_grant
www.instagram.com/dgauthor
www.pinterest.com/donnagrant1

64758582R00106

Made in the USA
Middletown, DE
17 February 2018